Waking The Weaver

A Timberhaven Novel

I0658483

Aaron Conaway

A K&Q Press Publication

Front Cover Photo Credit: Bobby Burch Photography

First Edition 2018

Preface

The road that led me to write *Waking The Weaver* is long and filled with stories, whose tellers made indelible marks on me and to whom the debt of thanks I owe can never properly be repaid. Among them:

To Dad, who gave me my love of reading.

To Mom, who taught me that not all great stories are told in a straight line.

To Chris Conaway, who would react to a song he loved with laughter and joy.

To Carrie Conaway Craig, who I told my first stories to and who I shared my earliest adventures with.

To Sarah Conaway Ross, the first fearless person I ever met.

To Daniel Moler and Jason Thrasher, my brothers, my oldest friends. We Warriors Three of Mount Vernon who have embarked on many adventures together, both in real life and at the table. That spirit lives in every story I tell.

To Dusty Dean, whose unceasing enthusiasm and interest in Timberhaven have helped me see this book through.

To Matt Howard and Joanie, who gave this book a read when it was mostly scribbles.

To Bobby Burch and Hannah Arredondo, for helping me with this book's cover.

And to Lauren Conaway, my beloved bride, my Bella. Brilliant, beautiful, and ambitious. The copilot of all my adventures and dreams, whose love and support made all of this possible.

Timberhaven was born eight years ago to the day of my writing this Preface (2-15-2018), of misfit characters and story ideas that I didn't know what to do with. It wasn't until I put them all into one small town that things started to click for me. There's science fiction here, yes. And fantasy. But among all of the weirdness and the mystery, the darkness and the goofy, there's whimsy and hope.

Timberhaven can be a dangerous place, true. But it's a place of wonder at its heart.

I hope you enjoy your time here.

- Aaron Conaway

The children always followed. The fair came with rules, it knew. Rules that the children, with their bubblegum laughter and cotton-candied little faces, were told beforehand – keep in mommy's sight. No running off. Beware of dangerous men, with their big, dark coats and nasty teeth. So it kept in colors. Vivid, let's have some fun! colors. No coats. Sparkling eyes, perfect teeth. Prizes and treats. And the children always followed.

~~*The demon danced in the trees*~~   *Demon? Research alt. monsters.*

From the journal of one Michael Gideon:

June 17, 2010

I've finally unpacked the rental car. It took much longer than it should have, for my only having brought a closet's worth of clothes, some books, and my typewriter with me, but Timberhaven is a . . . it's an interesting place. I was a little preoccupied.

Lord, I haven't written in a journal in years. Good penmanship isn't my area of expertise, but I thought it might help break the block when I'm stuck, get the juices flowing. And I can't deny it, I'm stuck. Page 128 and I still don't know what *Chaos*

Fair is actually about or where it's going. Patty's left four messages just today and I don't know what to tell him, but luckily the cell service is terrible out here so my "missing calls" isn't that far-fetched.

So I'll drink my bourbon, smoke my cigar and write in my journal, much like I imagine Hemingway did when he was stuck. Only I'm not sitting in a lawn chair on the beach in Cuba.

Timberhaven, man, this place is wild. It's gorgeous and bleak all at the same time. It seems to be surrounded by forest – making its name make sense – and I'm digging that. I really feel like I'm off the radar here, which should be helpful, but it's strange. Some of the trees here are what I think the trees in Oz – not the trees that talked, but maybe their neighbors – were like; enchanted with a sense of purpose – of function.

Well, that certainly sounds . . . stupid. Let us have another bourbon dear Evey, what say you? No? Just me then. Don't mind if I do.

The first person I met here was Audrey. Audrey Fell. She's a colorful, eccentric, girl. Her father owns and runs The Fell Hotel along with some rental properties in town. This house included. She helped out a bit by pointing me around town to the necessities: post office, grocery store, that sort of thing. Over the course of one afternoon, I saw her in three different theatrical hats and, though I met her as a brunette, I saw her a second time with streaks of red in her purple hair. And she seems to know everybody here, particularly in the area that the locals call the Village; an artist colony of sorts that blends with local peddlers and what looks to be Timberhaven's homeless set. I couldn't believe the number of tents and lean-tos I saw in what most small towns would call their square. She showed me Shadow Lake, with its rowboats to be borrowed and fishing nets to be lent, and where a group of mimes was performing Andrew Lloyd Webber's *Cats* in a small, stone amphitheater at the lake's edge. It was a crazy walk around town.

I'm now looking out the window and across the roughly two acres between us at my neighbor, Hurd. Audrey told me his name. He's another part of why I call this town interesting. It's just after six in the morning as I write this. The sun is only now coming up through the trees behind his house and Hurd, this little old man, he's eighty if a day, has been doing some sort of – I actually don't know what to call it. It's almost a dance. Like tai chi mixed with some sumo stances all set to a jungle rhythm that only he seems to hear. But he's been at it since I sat down to write, at around nine o'clock last night. He's just circling his house, over and over. The man has endurance, I'll give him that.

I haven't officially met him yet, him or his wife, Angela. She waves at me pleasantly, though, whenever she catches me coming in and out of the house. Much like any loving grandmother I've ever heard of. She seems like the apron-wearing cookie-baking type, what with the way the kids around here seem to flock to their house. Hurd hasn't even acknowledged my being over here, though, sticking to whatever routine he has and going about his business with his head down. When he's not doing his "bring forth the sun" dance, or whatever that is.

He's gone inside now. I can just make out Angela through their kitchen window, making coffee.

Better get back to it – the cadence, the clickety-clack of the typewriter – or just go to sleep if I'm not going to accomplish anything else here.

I need to move that mirror off the wall. There's a mirror across from where I've set up shop here in the living room and I keep glancing over at it, trying to catch what's attracting my attention over there. So far, it's just my reflection. God, look at me. I'm a mess. I look like a heavier Patrick Bergin without the mustache, if he'd been slapped around with a bugle.

Looks like it's bedtime, after all, Evey.

We'll try the real writing again tonight.

* * * * *

11:15 a.m.

I slept for maybe five hours.

I woke up with an unknown tune humming in my head. At least so far as I could tell, I *think* it was in my head. I was in that place where you're only dreaming that someone punches at you or that you're falling off a step stool, but your body physically reacts to it like it's actually happening. Regardless, it sounded like someone was humming from somewhere in the living room. So much so that I actually sat up on the couch (I was so tired, I never made it to my bed this morning), and sought out the origin of the serenade. Nobody was around.

I've got to quit smoking cigars so close to bedtime . . .

I tried to sit down and do some work, but all I came up with to type was:

YOU ARE A NO TALENT HACK

I debated on whether to hyphenate "no-talent" or to go with loser instead of hack but then decided that the entire exercise wasn't very productive, prudent or not, and took a shot of vodka to clear my head. Tempt my muse from her hiding place as it were. Since I'm back to writing here, though, it seems she's once again a no-show.

I'm going to clean up a bit and go walk around town.

*   *   *   *   *

3:45 p.m.

Today I met a man named Thegan.

He's a giant of a man, with dark skin and dark eyes. If I didn't know better, I'd say that the Chargers were playing some covert game in town and that I was talking to Shawne Merriman, in disguise, and with infinitely bushier hair.

Thegan is huge.

I met up with him as I wandered around the Village. Here was this colossus walking the streets in a dark blue, 80s-style puffy vest, jean shorts, and sandals all the while reading (and I still can't believe it, stumbling upon such an obscure pick), Chaucer's *The House of Fame*. Just slowly meandering about as he turned the pages. Imagine if you will, Evey, that my garage had taken up the habit of going out for after dinner strolls and you'd just about have him perfectly envisioned.

I stopped him walking into a low-hanging branch – well, low-hanging for him – and not long afterward we sat down, right there in the dirt street alongside the pub, and compared notes about what we'd been reading lately: he, a novel pertaining to Chechen scholars of the 15th century establishing a philosophical bend toward urban lore while contending with increasingly heavy lupine activity on the borderlands, and I, *Maybe It's Just Gas: A Guide To Getting Around Writers Block*. So he won that little contest.

Just as I got up and invited Thegan into the pub for some of the Village's finest liquid discussion, Ms. Fell came, reminding Thegan of a meeting that they had established earlier in the week where she would get to plaster cast his hands (hands, once she pointed them out, I noticed could crush my head like it was nothing if he so chose) for an art project, and he made to leave with her.

I then had a conversation that played out like this. I mention it here both because I can use the practice of writing my dialog and it's a way to return to the oddness of the conversation later.

"Oh, Ms. Fell?" I shouted to her as they started to round the corner of the pub.

"Please, it's Audrey."

"Of course, Audrey. You didn't by chance happen by the rental house today, did you?"

"No, why?"

"It's just that I thought — no, I could have *sworn* that I heard someone humming a song while I was sleeping. It was probably just a dream, but it occurs to me now that it was a woman's voice."

At my mentioning it, Audrey smiled at me and said, "Ah, yes. You are my lady."

"Um . . . excuse me?"

"Freddie Jackson's *You Are My Lady*. That was the song you heard."

I didn't have much of a response, or at least none came quickly enough before:

"Glad I could help, Mr. Gideon!" and Audrey was off with Thegan.

I forgot to even go inside the pub, I was so confused. I just came back to the rental house and wrote all of this down.

I need a nap.

*   *   *   *   *

June 18, 2010

It's a little after midnight as I write this. My "nap" seems to have gotten away from me.

My head is killing me. Gonna grab something to wash it down.

Odd.

This note was taped to the front door:

Dear Sir,

I have not made your acquaintance as of yet and would very much like to remedy that. My name is Salme Nicoline and I would consider it a personal favor if you could attend a little engagement at my cottage on Sunday evening, June the twentieth, at seven o'clock sharp. Simply follow the small path that runs from behind the post office in town and you won't be able to miss it. I apologize for the last minute invitation, but I am a traditionalist. Antiquated though the practice may be, I always check my well for assurances, regardless of what the wind whispers. I look forward to our meeting and I'm sure the others will as well.

Cordially,

Ms. Salme Nicoline

I'm taping this here as proof of just how weird this place gets. Who does this? First I've got some ghost humming songs at me (which I haven't forgotten about and in fact just got goosebumps all over, though I don't even believe in . . . whatever all of that is. I think I need to have a sit down with Audrey. At least I don't hear any Freddie whoever tonight) and now some well-watching old lady gets a tip from the wind that I should come hang out with her and her bridge buddies. (I mean bridge the card game, of course, but it occurs to me that here in Timberhaven, bridge buddies could take on an entirely different meaning.)

Where's a Billy Goat Gruff when you need one.

And I lost another day of writing! I can't keep ignoring Patty forever and I've got nothing new to show since our last phone call. Not any real work.

There's Hurd, out in the yard doing his thing.

Distractions, distractions, distractions. Maybe renting this house wasn't such a good idea after all.

That's it. I'm going to finish this cigar and knock out a chapter.

*   *   *   *   *

3:16 a.m.

Three hours later and nothing. ~~My muse, my . . . talent has dried up and died, flushed away in a deluge of excess. I'm a failure.~~

My process is all muddled up for some reason. It's like leaving to go on a cross-country road trip and reaching into the key bowl to find a handful of marshmallows where your car keys should be.

I just need to relax. Deep breaths. It will come.

Bourbon shot. Use the shot glass to catch the little bit that seeps out of my mouth. Mustn't waste the good stuff, not a drop.

I can't help but look at my note from Ms. Nicoline. Maybe I should start writing fantasy instead of horror. I could make a fortune here, what with all that goes on. And that's only what little I know about! Imagine if I researched some, poked around and explored the streets and woods a little. I bet there are all kinds of crazies here. My experience, little though it is, seems to suggest so.

I'm going to do one more shot and then throw my shoes on and go for a walk.

Here's hoping none of these psychos are armed.

*   *   *   *   *

Something is . . . off.

I woke up on the front steps of my house at around nine this morning, completely filthy. Like I'd been dropped into a big barrel of leaves, shaken, and then unceremoniously dumped into a bog.

But that's not what feels so strange. I've certainly been hungover before, and this feeling is nowhere near the same zip code as that. I can't quite put my finger on it, but my head feels different. It's not just that my headache is gone either. I feel lighter.

I felt like someone was watching me as I showered. I even checked – twice – to make sure there was no one standing outside of the shower curtain. There wasn't. I didn't even hear any humming. Audrey Fell's story needs some fine-tuning or I'm going to be jumping at everything around here.

My morning routine was shot. I couldn't finish my first cigar of the day – what I jokingly refer to as my Igniter – putting it out after the third drag. Then I opted to drink a glass of straight orange juice instead of my typical Bloody Mary because the Bloody Mary tasted sour in my mouth.

What is wrong with me?

I reread my last entry to see if anything there would help. Nope. I was just grumping a lot. Pretty dark headspace, I guess. There was nothing there to help me piece the last nearly ten hours together, though.

I don't remember much after heading out the door this morning. Nothing seems to be physically wrong with me, so I'm pretty sure I didn't get sauced and into a fight or anything. My wallet was still on me when I woke up on the steps, all my cash and cards in it, so I wasn't mugged. I was just dirty and really worn out.

I do remember dreaming of bizarre, powerful images, though. Hideous tree-men – creatures with bark skin, tree branch hair and moldy peach pit eyes. A nightclub with stained glass windows; Thelonious Monk playing in the background. A gray cat, striding wherever it pleased, and a stern knight, adorned in brilliant, white-light armor.

That's quite a brain full of imagery to pick up in such an unobtrusive-looking town. Outside of the trees and all of the tents in the Village – and some of their occupant's wares – there's not a lot of color here in Timberhaven. So, either I drunkenly stumbled into the most fantastic prop shop this side of Hollywood last night or I am waaay too stressed about *Chaos Fair*.

I'm looking out my window at Angela, puttering around her yard. I don't think I've ever seen her leave the house, outside of working in her flower garden in their yard. Maybe Hurd is old school, not letting his woman far from the home fires.

Huh. That's strange. I just waved at Angela, but she didn't respond with her usual pleasant smile and wave back. She just turned around and walked back into her house.

God, I hope I didn't do anything embarrassing last night. Why can't I remember anything after putting on my shoes?

Great. As if on cue, someone's knocking at the front door. . .

*   *   *   *   *

I wonder if I can get my deposit back from Mr. Fell.

I answered the door to find a group of small children wearing dark red robes, their hoods pulled up like tiny scarlet monks in search of enlightenment, standing on my porch. The little one in front – there were five altogether – had blonde, baby-doll ringlets peeking out from under the dark hood. She, I assume it was a little girl, held her hand up to me as if I should take it. The other four children stayed silent and unmoving, outwardly solemn in their lucidity.

And then they were simply no longer there.

I blinked and, instead, saw that Audrey was walking up my front steps, wondering aloud as to why I was standing and staring so strangely out my door.

"I – did you see any children out there? Just a second ago. Wearing. . ." I stopped my question short. The look on her face suggested that she hadn't seen any children, and that made me think that not sharing the midgets in monk robes might be the wiser course, conversationally speaking.

"Uh, kids? No." She peered around. "I don't see anyone but you. Are you okay?"

I assured her that I was, that the subject of my book, children snatched up by a supernatural evil, seemed to be wearing on me and that I was only tired. And that reminded me. . .

"Audrey, I'm afraid that I'm going to need you to further explain something to me. This, ahem, voice . . . this humming business. I'm going to need some clarification. You see, even though I don't believe in, in ghosts, or whatever, your story has me jumping at shadows. So, be straight with me, what's going on?"

"I never said she was a ghost. Dorthea won't – can't hurt you. She, oh it's just so very sad. I kinda thought that you staying here might, however crazy the thought might be, make things easier for her. She's a writer too, well, a poet. Outside of that, I'm afraid that it's not my story to tell."

"Slow down, Audrey, you're speaking very quickly."

"I'm sorry. I do that sometimes."

Audrey has a way of making my head spin while I'm talking to her. I tried to steer her back to some more of my questions, as her answer had only led to more of them, when she hit me with another shift in conversational lanes.

"So, what gift are you going to bring to the Gathering at Lady Nicoline's? Might I suggest – if you don't mind the suggestion – that you bring figs? Lady Nicoline loves a nice assortment of figs. But don't bring anything made of iron because she wouldn't thank you for that. My friend Wesley, he's a painter, he brought her a – he paints paintings, you understand, not, like, houses or anything – anyway, Wesley went to a Gathering when we were kids, I was ten and he was twelve – I didn't get invited – and he brought Lady Nicoline an old horseshoe – he only meant it as lucky and besides, he didn't know any better, not like I might have, but boy he does now! Lady Nicoline, she wouldn't even touch it! She just spit three times and said" – here she flourished her hands and spun around, hopping up on my porch step – "'Master Bells,' because, well, that's Wesley's last name, 'for the whole of a decade, you will not be able to see any color found in rainbows!' which is bad for an artist, really. But he fooled her. All his stuff is in black and white. Well, at least for the next two years until the curse is over. Then, he and I are going to . . . wait, where was I heading with this?"

I stammered a bit, Evey, I won't lie. I was actually only able to recall a fraction of all that she said, so as to write it down here.

"I . . . Audrey, thank you for the advice. I'm not even sure I'm going to attend this gathering."

"It's not just a gathering, but a Gathering. You're not saying it right. Lady Nicoline only has one every so often, only when something important happens. Likely none of her other Gatherings were for anything nearly as important as what this one is for if the stories are true. Um, I can't talk about this. You'll see if you go." And then Audrey turned to go. She's always heading off somewhere.

Honestly, I've not decided if I care or not about this gathering at Ms. Nicoline's, so I let it drop. I did manage one last question before she left.

"Audrey. The humming. I don't hear it anymore. Only that one time, so –"

"Oh, yeah, you wouldn't have heard it again yet, would you? It's not Thursday!"

I really shouldn't have bothered asking.

I wonder if I *need* my deposit back from Mr. Fell. . .

*   *   *   *   *

June 18, 2010-June 19, 2010

It's almost midnight.

After Audrey left this morning, I went for a walk in an attempt to clear my head. It didn't help much. I still feel like I'm in a daze. Like driving in your car after it's been professionally detailed. It's your car, but it doesn't feel like it.

I've dealt with nothing but strange since coming here. My book is no closer to being complete, the neighbors are . . . odd, to say the least, and now my booze doesn't taste right.

On my walk, I wandered around in the woods a bit. Just at the edge. Something there felt comfortable. Nice. Like a dream that you try and hold tight to just as it's slipping away when you wake. I don't know what that feeling is, or was, and it was only fleeting, but I enjoyed it.

As I headed out of the woods, I met a man fishing in a small pond. He stood barefoot in the water, using a tent pole to fish with what looked to be a string from a tennis racquet as line and green olives as bait. As I approached, this man, I never got his name, without looking up from his task, asked me if I was the writer.

"I guess I am." (Small town insight that I've gleaned: everyone knows your line of work within minutes of your arriving.)

"Could you make me up a story right quick?" he asked, not looking up from his cast, "I've got a tab to pay down to Cal's."

"I – sorry –" I wondered what Cal's was. "I can't just now. I've got too much on my mind." He nodded and plopped another olive-covered hook into the pond while I went on my way.

Should I find it worrisome that I'm beginning to find situations like this less absurd than I might have at one time?

I'm not sure what's going on here in Timberhaven, with me or any of its inhabitants. Speaking of which – no, Hurd's not in his yard doing his dancing routine. Wonder what's going on there. Their house is dark. Granted, it's after midnight, too.

I know what you're thinking, Evey: "Good Lord, Mikey, it's late and they're both old. Of course they're in bed!" When did I become Gladys Kravitz?

It's this place, this land. It's almost magical, dumb as that sounds. It's . . . soothing. Comforting. Something is happening to me here, and I don't understand it. But I will. And I think I know where to start finding some answers.

I've just made up my mind to attend Ms. Nicoline's party.

*　　*　　*　　*　　*

June 19, 2010

9:15 a.m.

I didn't sleep well last night. I tossed and turned until after five, and when I did sleep, uncomfortable dreams wrecked any chance of rest. One took place in the middle of a moonless night. I was wandering a flat, lifeless field, all alone – lost, yet in search of something. I don't know what I was looking for or why, but I was so unnerved by the dream upon waking.

Remember when we were kids, Evey? How I used to have those nightmares? I can't even remember what they were about now. But I do remember how I'd run to your room and jump into your bed crying. You'd make me a bowl of cereal, no matter what time it was, and calm me down. Tell me how nightmares were just my imagination's way of taking things I'd learned or seen that day and flipping them around in my brain, seeing what made them tick.

My imagination is working a little overtime, I guess, given its diet of weird things to digest around here. Too bad none of it is helping me with *Chaos Fair*.

God, I'm craving scrambled eggs and black coffee. Some toast, with strawberry jam and butter. And a newspaper to read. Some normalcy. Waking up at such random times lately seems to be wrecking my eating schedule. Regardless, there's nothing in the fridge but orange juice, Bloody Mary fixings, and pears. (When did I buy pears?)

There's a diner in town, Sally's Place. Think I'll go see how the locals do breakfast.

*   *   *   *   *

12:30 p.m.

Well, I never made it to the diner.

On my way there I thought I'd look at what I was getting myself into if I did go to this gathering, so I walked by the post office to look at Ms. Nicoline's place.

I had just made out the little path that she'd mentioned in her note when my attention was drawn to the lot behind the Post Office. It was empty, or so I thought, except for one structure – what can only generously be described as a shack – which gave a precarious lean near the back of the lot.

In front of the shack, sitting on a stack of magazines with his back to me, was a man wearing a sort of hat constructed out of a gallon milk jug. A few little wisps of silver hair stuck out through holes in the plastic while the rest of his mane tucked under what appeared to be a patchwork green overcoat. I could hardly make out just what but he was yelling something.

"No, no, no! How do you ever hope to perform for anyone if you don't take your lessons seriously?"

As I carefully approached, investigating further, I saw that he appeared to be berating an opossum at his feet, a squirrel in his lap, and a robin that was hopping around his "hat".

"Domingo, you can't let Carreras overpower you. Your voices are to blend. Blend! And Pavarotti, don't think that I haven't noticed your slacking down there. I am surrounded by undisciplined layabouts!"

I asked if everything was okay, and the gentleman turned to face me. His look was intense.

"What is it?!"

At his shout, the robin took to the sky while the opossum and squirrel ran for the shack.

"Rehearsal is not over, you know!" he yelled, standing slowly and shaking his fist at the fleeing animals. "Okay, okay. Take five. Domingo, no! You've had your breakfast, you naughty squirrel." He sighed and then turned back to me, his face had softened. "Carreras won't be back in five, you know. Birds have such a terrible sense of priority. I don't believe we've officially met yet. My name is Lord Jarboe" – he took my hand, shaking it – "proprietor and sole custodian of Tater Town." He spread his other hand, the one not shaking mine as if to guide my eyes to our surroundings.

"Tater Town?" I asked.

"Indeed! Heard of us, have you? How exciting! Mr. Gideon knows of Tater Town!"

"No, I meant – I only just –"

"I'd offer you some of our world-famous potato bits, but alas, this damnable heat wave we're currently suffering through has managed us too small a crop this season. I must always see to it that the villagers are fed first, lest the gypsies curse me."

I looked around his yard at the small mounds of dirt scattered all about as he straightened the milk jug on his head.

"Mr. Jack!" he yelled, his eyes searching our surroundings. "You've not seen my helper anywhere, have you? Purple suit? Bowler hat?"

"No, sorry. Just you."

"Mr. Jack, I need you!" he yelled again to the empty lot and then sighed. "Well, no matter. If you happen to see him, send him my way, will you? He's quite mad, you know, but don't let that worry you, he's harmless. Good help is so hard to find."

I had to wonder at what being crazy looked like to this guy.

"Heavy is the crown in this dark age." he continued. "Makes a body wonder why we try sometimes, and not just chuck it all in and buy a boat. There's good fishing, on a boat. Or, well, from a boat, at any rate. If, of course, you don't mind all of the sharks." He readjusted his plastic crown again, blinking rapidly as he looked nervously around at the ground. I noticed his eyes, then. He has one dark green eye, one intense blue.

"Well, I didn't mean to be a bother. I just heard the yelling and thought I'd make sure nothing was wrong." I made to leave.

"No bother, no bother at all! I'll be seeing you tomorrow then? At the Gathering?"

This caught my attention.

"At Ms. Nicoline's place? Do you know her?" I thought I might finally get some straight answers. Granted, they'd be coming from the guy in the milk jug hat, so maybe not *straight* answers . . .

"Of course! We lords and ladies all know one another. She resides in the neighboring sovereignty." He pointed down the little path in front of his, well, his town. "This will be my first official Gathering though. It's merely been political niceties before now. Oh well, best get back to it. These lads of mine won't practice if I don't make them." And with that, Jarboe headed back into his shack of crooked boards and duct tape before I could ask anything further of him.

Just then my cell rang. It was Patty, finally allowed by the cell phone gods to check up on me. I lied to him about the status of *Chaos Fair* every step of the way back here to the house.

Guess I'd better at least try to put something down.

*   *   *   *   *

I'm making some headway today on the book, twenty solid pages and counting. It's about a quarter to four now. Think I'll take a little break, head out on the porch and have one of those pears I don't remember buying. Weird or not, it's been a productive day. Patty should be happy. I guess I should be thinking about what to take to Ms. Nicoline's get together since I've decided to go. I just flipped back a few pages to see what it was that Audrey said would make a nice gift. This journal keeping has come in handy, Evey!

*　　*　　*　　*　　*

6:48 p.m.

So, I just had my first real conversation with Angela. I think I need a second before I get into this.

I was out on the front porch, eating my pear and looking over some typed pages. I – I don't know what made me look, but I looked toward Hurd and Angela's place to find Angela standing at the edge of their property, looking at me. Her blue dress billowing in the breeze reminded me, Evey, of sailing the Cape in the summer when we were kids. Her silver hair was loose around her shoulders. She held her hands out to either side of her as if preparing to feed cartoon bluebirds out of them.

"I was once an actress, you know." She said to me.

Caught up in my childhood memory of the Cape as I was, she continued, seemingly unaffected by my lack of response,

"But that was a very long time ago. I enjoyed it though, being part of the arts. I was a foolish girl giving it up like I did."

I walked over to her, apologizing for staring as I offered my hand to formally introduce myself. I needn't have bothered.

"Yes, Mr. Gideon, I know who you are. You're new to town. A gifted artist, if not self-confident in your gift. I'm familiar with your type."

"Have I somehow offended you?" I asked, recalling privately the waking up on my front steps incident. "If so, for whatever reason, I apologize."

"I'm far too difficult to offend at my age, Mr. Gideon. Have no concern on that front. No, no, I'm merely letting this business with my husband affect my opinion of you, and for that, I apologize."

I was confused. I haven't had any contact with Hurd. "How is your husband? I haven't seen him around."

"And you shan't, I'm afraid. He will be laid up for some time. Not surprising, given what happened. Not that you should feel guilty. My husband has a mind of his own."

Thoroughly mystified, that's what I was. Before I could ask what in God's name she was talking about, asking carefully in light of the Alzheimer's she was clearly suffering from, she continued,

"Mr. Gideon, I have a boon to ask of you, though I cannot ask it without first knowing that your answer will be yes. Will you do me this kindness?"

I said I would. I didn't figure it could hurt, helping a woman of Angela's years out. I really am a stupid man.

"As Hurd is unable to attend Lady Nicoline's Gathering, and I cannot go in his place, I need you to speak in favor of the third matter to be decided upon. A proxy for me, you understand."

"I really don't."

"Forgive me, I was being polite. Your understanding the matter is completely irrelevant, Mr. Gideon, so long as your lack of understanding is in no way indicative of an inability to nod your head."

I hadn't been dressed down in such a way since college. I felt like I did when I got caught going through the cool stuff in Grandma's attic without permission.

"Have we reached an accord, Mr. Gideon?"

"I say yes, as *your* fill-in vote, on the third topic of conversation. I really – I'm just renting the house for a few weeks. I don't think, I mean, if there's some sort of housing committee issue going on, I can't imagine that I'll be part of that. Truth be told, I don't understand why I even got invited to this thing."

"'This thing?'" She seemed very put off by me at that point. "Mr. Gideon, I assure you, 'this thing', as you so aptly refer to it, changes everything and should not be entered into lightly. Though, as I talk to you, I'm not sure that I understand your invitation either. Good day, sir."

And she walked back to her house, leaving as quietly as she'd come.

What *is* this Gathering?

* * * * *

June 20, 2010

I worked until around three this morning and got fifty more pages done! I even got past the hurdle that's been blocking me, of why the demon at the fair was targeting children. Something certainly has my creative juices flowing.

Maybe it's the pears.

Damn, that reminds me, I've got to find some figs somewhere for the party tonight. Maybe the Village will have something. Wow. I'm still not sure that going to see Mr. Fell for my deposit back wouldn't be my wisest course of action, but I admit, I've become enchanted by this place. Yes, it's been creepy at times. Frustrating, too. (And I've not even been here an entire week.) But tiptoeing amongst brass bidet-framed velvet Elvises while a 45 of "The Eggplant That Ate Chicago" plays from the back of a neighboring tent, all in an attempt to shop a caravan of wandering wild children for fruit; this is how I'll spend my afternoon. Figs, mind you, that I'll be giving as a gift to the hostess of a gathering – sorry, Gathering, of locals who will be having a vote of some kind at which I, in the role of substitute vote for my possibly (probably) mad neighbor, am to answer in the affirmative to the third topic.

God, I'm starting to write like Audrey Fell talks. Patty would just love that.

Okay, the mirror in the living room is being funky again. I feel stupid writing you this, Evey, but I can't shake the feeling that something beneath that polished surface isn't right. Like it's a mirror, but not a mirror. I just touched it, going so far as to need proof that it wouldn't shimmer away. My smudged fingerprints would suggest otherwise, but I think I'll finish this entry in the kitchen anyway.

*   *   *   *   *

Well, I didn't have much else to write this morning, so instead, I got out of the house.

Stupid mirror.

It's around five o'clock now, only two hours until I need to be at Ms. Nicoline's place.

I found some figs in the Village, but I couldn't pick them up. You see, it turns out that figs, wild figs, at any rate, are sort of a rare commodity here in Timberhaven and can only be bartered for through one source: the Pinleys.

I'm going to try and put down here exactly how events played out, but it's a lot to follow:

- Mr. and Mrs. Pinley had figs on hand. Seven figs, precisely. But, and this was fun to discover, money is of no use in the Village. Everybody uses a bartering system. As it turns out, the Pinleys are pretty damn proud of their figs. I offered to make up a story for them, but they said that they were all set on new tales. In talking to them, however, I discovered that Mr. Pinley has quite a sweet tooth, especially for the peanut butter fudge of a local psychic named Brynne, a.k.a. Madam Xaxu. Unfortunately, Mrs. Pinley thinks that Mr. Pinley stares at Madam Xaxu a bit overlong whenever he's around her, and so, has banned Mr. Pinley from seeing her. Mr. Pinley, after pulling me aside, suggested that he would be willing to part with the figs if I could bring him some of Madam Xaxu's fudge.

- After finding Madam Xaxu's tent and then locating her by Mr. Pinley's description of "fire-kissed hair" (and seeing why he might have stared, allegedly), I asked if I could barter for some of her peanut butter fudge. (At this point, I was wishing that I had had more on me than a pack of gum and my fingernail clippers since the contents of my wallet had proven useless.) She said that she did have some fudge and would be willing to let me have it for a song. Literally, she wanted me to sing, in key, any song I'd like so long as it had been a radio hit in 1952. As I can't sing a note, and I told her so, I offered instead to make up a tale for her. She politely declined, claiming to be all set on stories at the moment, too, but said that she really loved Thegan's voice and would be willing to trade me the fudge if he sang to her.

 - I found Thegan sitting by himself, writing in his journal. I asked him if he would mind singing to Brynne for me. He told me that he would love to, but that, though he would have liked to do it as a favor, he'd have to barter with me so as to not disrupt the system. I offered, yet again, to tell a tale. Nope. (Thegan explained that everyone had been fully stocked up with new stories thanks to someone named Mahin filling the coffers, as it were. Ain't that always the way?) He wanted, after thinking long and hard on it, to play a game of chess with Lord Jarboe.

- Jarboe was in his garden, or Tater Town, I suppose, when I went to find him. He was using a makeshift garden spade – made out of a pool cue with what looked to be a metal protractor wired to the end – to hunt . . . I'm not actually sure what it was he was hunting, but Jarboe kept yelling. "Get away with you! I don't wish to find a wig's worth of hair has grown out of my left nostril come morning!" and chopping at the ground. Once I got him to calm down enough to ask about the chess game with Thegan, he said he'd be happy to. For a *Superman* comic book.

I'm here to tell you, nobody in the Village has any comic books, *Superman* or otherwise. And trust me, I spent as much time as I could to look for one. But that's what Jarboe wanted. He wouldn't be moved. So, since I couldn't pull a *Superman* comic out of thin air, Thegan didn't get his chess game. Which meant no song for Madam Xaxu, nor peanut butter fudge for Mr. Pinley. Which, in turn, meant no figs for me. Thank you for shopping, but try again tomorrow.

I ended up stopping by the grocery store and buying a package of Fig Newtons. Hopefully, they will work. With the way this day has gone on the produce front, I'm not holding out much hope though.

Off to Ms. Nicoline's.

*   *   *   *   *

June 22, 2010

Lady Nicoline. Ms. Nicoline. Either way, Salme Nicoline? Yeah, she's a man. Turned out that we'd already met in person, too. She/he was the guy I met who was fishing in the pond during my walk in the woods on Friday. But that wasn't the only surprise waiting for me at this Gathering. . .

I needed a few days to let the events of Sunday sink in before getting this down. Thank God I thought to take my tape recorder. I'm good at remembering details, but there's no way I could have retained all of the information being thrown around.

There were eight of us present: me, Lady Nicoline as "herself", Jarboe, Thegan, Brynne (aka Madam Xaxu), and three others who would, over the course of the event, be introduced as

Sasha, Cade, and Mr. Trepp. We were seated around a long, oval-shaped wooden table in Lady Nicoline's backyard. Christmas lights were hung in and around the trees surrounding us, giving the entire event a fairytale feel.

This is the first time that I've played the tape back, and I'll begin transcribing it in a moment, just as I was told to do by Lady Nicoline.

I didn't record anything on the walk over. I met Jarboe as he exited Tater Town, and we walked toward Lady Nicoline's together. He was wearing his ever-present milk jug crown and had a worn out, plastic blue star pinned to his coat that faintly read, "First Place Speller!" We didn't talk much, though, as he was busy finishing one of his lessons; this time with Simone, a mouse that he had in his pocket.

Lady Nicoline met us at the gate to her backyard. I recognized immediately that I was looking at a man. He was clean-shaven, wearing a peasant dress and a woman's hat, but clearly wasn't trying to hide that she was a guy. At this point, I hadn't placed that we'd already met at the fishing pond.

Jarboe bowed deeply before Lady Nicoline and thanked her for his invite, crossing into the backyard by her leave. She then introduced herself to me and thanked me for coming.

I said I appreciated my invitation as well. As I did so, I started the tape recording in my pocket.

Lady Nicoline: "I'm sure you have so many questions about everything going on tonight, and I promise to answer those that I can, the best that I can. I must apologize once again for just leaving a note on your door and not introducing myself, but things have been very hectic for me as of late."

Me: "It was peculiar, but certainly not the oddest thing to happen to me this week."

Lady Nicoline: "Of that, I've no doubt. I hope the dreams are manageable."

Me: "How did – "

Lady Nicoline, to the gathered people: "Now that we've all arrived, let us sit. Would anyone like a beverage before we begin?"

Murmured acknowledgments one way or another. I filled a glass with iced tea from a red plastic pitcher.

Lady Nicoline: "Good, good. Now, introductions."

Huh. That's weird. At this point, I should hear Mr. Trepp say that he's a busy man and couldn't they just get on with things. I remember him saying something to that effect. He's not on the tape, though. I've rewound and played it back three times and all I hear are background noises – my ice clinking in the glass as I drink – until:

Lady Nicoline: "Be that as it may, Mr. Trepp, the rules will be adhered to. We'll start with you since you're in such a rush. Who have you brought to my table?"

Once again, I have no recording of Mr. Trepp's voice, but I can hear that the tape recorded while he was speaking. Great, like he didn't creep me out enough already.

I went to Hollywood a few years back. It was the first time one of my books was being shown around for a possible movie adaptation, and my then agent – this is before Patty – thought that I should make the rounds, put my name out there. I hated it, the fakeness of it all. Anyway, while I was there, I met with multiple producers, assistant producers, etc., guys in their thirties who didn't even bother trying to remember why they were shaking my hand, having already mentally checked-out and headed to their next meeting.

Mr. Trepp had their look, if not their feel. They'd been pups, growling and barking into cell phones and at fresh-faced PAs to prove they could be heard. Mr. Trepp was a wolf. When he smiled, I felt it in my jugular.

He introduced Sasha, his assistant. She looked like candy wrapped in a bear trap. Sweet to taste but you'd lose a hand in the attempt.

Then he announced his candidate for Timberhaven's replacement Weaver, Cade. I wasn't positive what a Weaver did in Timberhaven, but if Cade was any indication it wasn't pleasant. He's a built guy, maybe mid-twenties. He has more tattoos than any three people I know and that was only the count from the skin I could see. He has a shaved head, wore a dog collar, and has brilliant white, perfectly straight teeth. He has the most unsettling pair of eyes I've ever seen.

After introducing Cade, Mr. Trepp searched around the table and said that he saw no other worthwhile candidates and asked if it was safe to assume that Cade had the job.

Jarboe/Thegan speaking over one another: "I say, it is not!/Proper protocol, sir!"

Mr. Trepp merely smiled, looking around the table at each of us. I literally averted my eyes as he turned toward me.

Lady Nicoline: "As it happens, we do have another candidate. Mr. Gideon? Would you be so kind as to accept the nomination?"

Me: "I, uh, I'm not sure that –", I remember finding the nerve to glance at Mr. Trepp. He was still smiling.

Lady Nicoline: "It's merely a formality. You've seen how we in Timberhaven have our eccentricities so far as formalities go. We just need a suitable vote. We couldn't have Master Cade run unopposed."

Mr. Trepp was still staring, smiling his wolf smile at me like I was wearing a red hood.

Jarboe: "What say you?"

Me: "If, if it will help you all, sure. Sure, I'll be a candidate. Though I know nothing at all about weaving."

Thegan: "See! Ha-ha! See? I told you he'd do it."

Mr. Trepp never stopped smiling at me while he mentioned that I wasn't a resident of Timberhaven. Finally, he turned to speak to Lady Nicoline. (I'm still not able to hear his voice on the tape.)

Lady Nicoline: "Ah, but he is a resident. Only just, true, but that still counts. He currently does his work out of Fallenstar Manor."

Mr. Trepp nodded, turning to Sasha and Cade with his hands up. He said, "Looks like we'll be playing the game after all."

And then, we voted.

Even over all the sounds of the forest around us that night, I can hear my breathing start to quicken on the tape as the casting starts.

Ms. Nicoline was the first to stand.

"As the Voice of Three this evening, I, Salme, cast my vote for Michael. I feel Timberhaven can only benefit from his talent and I have faith in his strengths, as well as what he perceives as weaknesses. Samuel, however, remains unimpressed with Michael, having tried to secure a tale from him in the Western Woods only to be told no. His vote lies with Cade. Number One wishes to abstain, seeing the wisdom in neutrality."

That's when I figured out where I knew Ms. Nicoline's face from when she mentioned "Samuel" in the woods. I still don't really get the "Voice of Three" bit, if she suffers from MPD or something, but after she spoke her vote and took her seat again, the voting continued to her left, with Brynne.

"I sense fantastic promise in Michael. Even if he can't sing" – she had smiled at me – "he gets my vote."

As Brynne sat down, two dogs begin barking in the background on the tape. I was so wrapped up in the events of the table, I only vaguely remember it happening, but Jarboe is yelling on the tape, "Lincoln! Leopold! Stop that ruckus immediately!" Meanwhile, to Brynne's left, Thegan had risen to speak.

"Mr. Gideon – Michael – is my vote. He saw to my safety when I had no one else. He's a good friend and will make a fine Weaver." I have no idea what Thegan meant. I mean, I looked out for him when he was going to walk into that branch the other day, sure, but it's not like I gave him a kidney.

Wait. What was that?

Thegan was sitting right across from me, close enough that the tape seems to have caught him muttering something under his breath. Lemme try and rewind it. Maybe crank up the volume.

I can't be sure what he's saying entirely, but he definitely mentions "Dorthea" as he's sitting down.

In reading back through my entries, I see that that's the second time Dorthea's name has come up. Interesting.

Sasha stood next.

"Cade is an amazing talent. I could guarantee a solid sixteen percent increase in ad sales if I could have –"I remember that Mr. Trepp said nothing but had caught her gaze just here. "B-but he would be of fantastic use here in his hometown of Timberhaven. Help you guys out of your . . . bind. I vote for Cade."

Mr. Trepp stood before Sasha had even finished sitting down. He started speaking (yet again, I have no audio for him) about passion and proven mettle. It was pretty powerful, actually. Bit bizarre, too, but this whole thing was. He cast his vote for Cade, brandishing his arm toward him like a proud father.

Then Cade rose to speak. His eloquent speaking voice in no way matches his appearance.

"I am Timberhaven's Weaver. I've trained my entire life for it. Darkness holds no mystery for me, and so, can summon no fear. We have sat undefended for far too long. A situation I intend to remedy. I vote for myself."

Next up was Jarboe.

"I apologize, Lady Nicoline, for the disruption by the boys. Huskies are notorious for forgetting their manners. It's double lessons for you lot tomorrow!" he yelled the latter over his shoulder. "At any rate, I vote for Mr. Gideon. He's what we need here, I just know it."

It was at this point that the pressure was getting to be too much for me. I felt prodded and pushed. I didn't understand anything that was going on. Information was being thrown around at a mile a minute, things were going over my head, and I was just about done.

"Mr. Gideon?" Lady Nicoline said.

"Yes? Um, yes? Ah-ha, um. Yes. I don't really – that is, this is all just insane to me. I don't even know what I'm doing here."

I had looked around the table. Jarboe and Thegan looked hurt. Brynne, disappointed. Mr. Trepp smiled his toothy smile.

"Well, Mr. Gideon, it appears that you are breaking a tie in Timberhaven's vote for a Weaver," Lady Nicoline said, smiling, "and doing a fine job of it, might I add. I know that your mind must be positively racing with questions and doubts. You're no fool, after all. And you're not crazy. Dreams coming at you while you're asleep and awake, weird noises and neighbors, all when you had only come looking for a quiet place to do your work. It would fill anyone with nerves. But you're a writer. Even more so, a storyteller. A fly on the wall in every room you've ever been in, to better transform events therein into stories later."

Mr. Trepp spoke up at this point, attempting to interrupt Lady Nicoline, but she just went on.

"Well, sir, you are at the edge of another story. Curiosity has led you this far, but only a solid decision opens the next door. Do you say nay, thereby asking us to leave you to your work, alone and quiet in your rented home to finish your book? If that is your wish, you must only say so now and we will oblige. Or do you continue down the path that you've discovered and say yes, able to sate your curiosity on whatever comes next?"

And she was right. I had far too many questions. I'd go crazy without answers, and this might be the only way to continue collecting the pieces.

I voted for myself, with no idea of what I was accepting.

"Well then, that concludes the vote. Mr. Gideon, at a vote of five-four, is the new Weaver of Timberhaven," Lady Nicoline announced to all around the table. "Now, as the next bit of business is sensitive to town Titles, I'm afraid we must say good evening to you unbound citizens among us."

I didn't know whether I was to stay or go. Thegan motioned for me to stay seated. Brynne, Jarboe, Sasha, and Cade all left the backyard. Cade gave a cold stare my way as he left.

Once there were only four of us in earshot, Lady Nicoline continued,

"Good evening, Titles. Everyone has a full drink? Good. Let us begin with the second item to discuss this evening. Thegan?"

"Thank you. Ahem. We haven't had a Knight sighting since . . . the incident and the suffering has increased tenfold every day we go without a, well, a guard of some kind. Maybe a patrol?"

I had dreamt of a knight. A brilliant white came from his armor in the dream, almost as if it were plated in pure light.

"A knight sighting?" I'd asked the table. "I had a weird dream about a knight. And how did you know about my dreams, Ms. Nicoline? And guard what? Patrol? I can only take so much of this, this!" I admit now, I was feeling punch drunk from everything. My head was spinning. "I'm a Title, or a, a Weaver whatever, so I get it, you've got to tell this to me but, do it, yes, talk to me like, well, as if I'm a child. A child from another country – or no – a planet. Yeah, a small child from another planet. Someone, please."

"The Knight protects our borders from the things that wish us harm. He protects us as we sleep – protects our dreams. And he's missing," Thegan explained.

"The knight who protects your dreams is missing," I repeated, trying to better understand what madness tasted like. "I think, yes, this is my fault. When I said – you remember a moment ago? I said, 'Speak to me like a small, alien child.' And I think perhaps maybe that concept is just too, well, um, you know, alien."

Do I sound like this? I speak like an idiot. Granted, dream-protecting knights being bandied about in adult conversation can throw a guy off, but still.

"Maybe you could just start from the beginning? For us newbies?" I asked Thegan.

"Oh, yes, sorry. You see, we here in Timberhaven – well, mostly in the Village and Old Town, not so much in the city proper – have grown accustomed to having a Knight protecting us as we sleep. He generally shows up in the dream when you're in the most danger. Most afraid. Some say – though there are others who reject this theory out of hand, allowing that there is no evidence to suggest that it's anything more than drink-induced hearsay" – Thegan had looked to Mr. Trepp – "but some claim that you can sometimes see the Knight *really* patrolling, outside of dreams. He's sometimes seen galloping on a steed. Other times he patrols on foot. I say it's possible, though I've not witnessed an appearance firsthand. Maybe it's an astral projection of some kind? If I knew whether he showed up as a corporeal presence, I could better decipher – well, look, I think I have some notes here. Let me show you –"

"Ahem. Thegan, I think that Mr. Gideon is finding this particular concept hard enough to grasp without reading any notes on the subject right now," Lady Nicoline said, bringing Thegan's attention from his satchel to her. "If he doesn't mind, maybe we could persuade Mr. Gideon to lunch with us later this week. Parson Leets has been maintaining the barrier quite well I think, considering the absence of the Knight. Perhaps he'll join us as well."

"Certainly! The Parson is doing a wonderful job. It was for his benefit that I had wanted to bring the topic up this evening. He's wearing himself too thin, I think. He could use the help. And we still don't know the outcome of the Knight. But yes, it could wait until we can explain things to Michael. I'll arrange everything after the Gathering."

At this point, Mr. Trepp suggested we move along to the third item we were meant to discuss. I remember his excitement, the tone of his voice changing, now that I think about it. Thegan, on the other hand, placed his satchel on his lap and shrunk back into his chair.

"Okay," Thegan nearly whispered. "We can move along to . . . to what comes next."

Mr. Trepp stood up. He slowly walked around the table, around all of us, continuing in his excited speech that Timberhaven had been through enough after recent events. That the burden of fixing and maintaining the barrier (I need, Evey, to find out more about whatever this is), especially with an unfamiliar as the Weaver (I remember mentally thanking him for the shot at my abilities even though, you know, I have no idea what they really are) was plenty on their plate. He was more than happy (I'd call it eager) to claim responsibility for this latest problem. Claim it, and take it with him.

Lady Nicoline quietly listened to Mr. Trepp until he finished speaking and sat back down. I noticed that she looked to Thegan from time to time during Mr. Trepp's speech.

"I see. You wish to take her with you. By rights, she should remain in Timberhaven, but this is a delicate matter, given . . . given the circumstances." She was looking to Thegan again, who in turn was absently latching and unlatching the satchel in his lap.

"Thegan?"

"I . . . do not ask this of me. I cannot – I will not see her stay here. Salme, look at what she is!" Thegan had tears in his eyes.

"Thegan, things need not be that way. She is merely potential here in Timberhaven. Her path no more decided than –"

"I will not see to her. That is my vote. Let Mr. Trepp take her." Thegan looked back down to his satchel.

"As you wish. We Three cannot take her either. Our nature would only serve to confuse her, and she is bound to be lost enough as it is. Though we think it an awful idea, I must vote for her to go with who will take her." Lady Nicoline looked down at the table.

I didn't like where this had headed. We were talking about a "her". Who would take *her*. What to do with *her*.

"What are you talking about? A person? Look, I don't know what's going on now, but –" I started.

Mr. Trepp and Thegan interrupted me. "Leave it alone, son," Mr. Trepp had said to me, though he's still not on the tape. "Please, Michael, you don't understand," Thegan pleaded.

Finally, Lady Nicoline stood up, giving little "hush" waves at us to quiet the two of them speaking at once.

"It seems, Mr. Trepp, that you may –"

"Wait a minute!" I said. Well, yelled, really. "I have a, I have something to say. Or, proclaim, as it were."

I could see that Lady Nicoline smiled slightly. Mr. Trepp did not.

"I am serving as a proxy vote for Hurd . . . uh, whatever his last name is. My neighbor, Hurd. Well, his wife Angela, actually. Who should be here to cast this vote themselves but, for whatever reason, can't."

"Michael, don't do this! Please!" Thegan yelled at me. "You don't understand! Regardless of what Salme says, she's evil! Evil is evil, no matter what side of the barrier you're on! You don't know what you'd be allowing here!"

I was taken completely off guard by Thegan's outburst. I thought maybe I should shut my mouth and let things play out as they may. Then I saw Mr. Trepp. He . . . I can't explain it very well here. With words, I mean. I felt that Mr. Trepp *really* wanted whoever we were discussing to go with him, and, for reasons I don't understand, I couldn't let that happen.

"What is your vote, then, Mr. Gideon?" Salme asked.

"Well, understanding that it's not mine, but a proxy vote for Angela, I say yes. She can stay in Timberhaven."

Thegan quickly got up from the table and left Lady Nicoline's yard, ducking his enormous frame to avoid any Christmas lights that were hanging from the trees. Mr. Trepp leaned a bit back into his chair and nodded my way. I don't have it recorded, of course, but he said to me, "You seem to be keeping me from conducting my business, Mr. Gideon."

"We are all finished here, Mr. Trepp," Lady Nicoline said. "You may return to your hotel now."

"Don't I get to stay for the unveiling?" was the last thing I remember Mr. Trepp saying.

"The Gathering is over. Good night, Mr. Trepp," was all Lady Nicoline said to him as she started cleaning her table off.

Mr. Trepp smiled as he left the yard.

Lady Nicoline reached into the pocket of her dress once we were alone and handed me an envelope.

"And this is our last bit of business to attend this evening, Mr. Gideon." She kept talking as I opened the envelope. "I hope you will forgive Thegan's being upset. It's understandable, of course."

"You all have a tendency to speak in riddles, do you know that?" I fumbled with the envelope, trying not to rip whatever was inside. "What is this?"

"Yes, well, some minds prefer dot-to-dot puzzles, I know. Riddles are much more telling though, don't you think? About the asker of the riddle *and* the guesser. Any child can connect the dots until they see the picture of a boat or a horse. But a riddle, a good one, at any rate, can take you to unknown places as you try and work it out. Unlock parts of your mind that you had never used or had merely forgotten once you grew up. And what you have there, Mr. Gideon, by way and care of Angela, is the final piece to this particular riddle. But I must warn you, this riddle's answer leads to more questions, I'm afraid. Go home. Rest. Once you think you've got your mind around it, play back the tape you've had recording since your arrival – yes, I know all about it – and write everything down. I think you'll find that doing so might help you in your duties as Weaver."

I was embarrassed about the tape but tried to hide it.

"Yeah, uh, what about this Weaver business? What am I supposed to do?" I asked, pulling the note out of the envelope.

"We'll discuss everything at lunch. Your duties, questions, whatever you like. I'll leave another note on your door, seeing as that seems to work for you, with the particulars. Oh, and Michael? Thank you for the figs. They are my favorite. That Audrey Fell hears everything. Good night," she said, walking back into the house, her screen door slamming shut behind her.

I looked down at the note. In the little light left to me I could see that it had only one word written on it:

Corabeth.

I read it aloud.

The screen door burst open, and a little girl, maybe seven years old, stood before me, her black hair framing her pale white face like a doll's.

"I'd like to go home now," she told me.

Lady Nicoline turned her fairytale Christmas lights off.

*   *   *   *   *

June 23, 2010

It's Wednesday.

My first full week in Timberhaven is behind me. I just read over everything that's gone down since I showed up here and I gotta say, I sound . . . well, I don't sound okay.

But I'm *not* crazy. I'm looking out the living room window right now at proof that things have played out just as I've described here. Angela is watching from her porch as little Corabeth runs all over the yard, chasing what appear to be butterflies.

Corabeth said very little at first, during our walk home the other night. She kept stopping and looking back at the way we had come like she was anticipating something.

"What is it?" I asked, peering along the tops of the tree line just as she was. Short of a semi-full moon coming up, I didn't see anything.

"I'm looking for Thayne. He's up there, but I haven't made him out yet," she told me, her eyes darting all over the sky.

"Oh, I see," was all I could come up with. I'm not very good with children.

"You should not be so demissive, I think. Dragons do not take very kindly to that." She actually almost glared at me as she said it.

"Well, then, tell your dragon I'm sorry. I meant no offense. And I think you meant dismissive. That's an awfully big word for a little kid."

"That's because I am *not* a little kid. I'm almost seven, I'll have you know. Though" – she looked somewhat lost – "I really don't remember much about being six." I felt sorry for her, though I was way out of my depth so I just hurried us along to Hurd and Angela's place.

When we were about a block away, I could see that Angela was waiting for us in her front yard. Corabeth was looking just beyond the house to the trees, listening as the wind danced through them. Once we got to Angela's fence line, Corabeth looked up at her.

"I like your forest. Do any monsters live there? I have a dragon named Thayne. He likes to catch monsters. He cuts them to ribbons and gobbles them up! Does the moon always shine so brightly here? I heard a song once, about a lady who lives in the moon. She sings a birthday song while the moon hides, and a . . . some other kind while the moon is bright. I guess the moon doesn't like birthdays, but I do and mine is coming up! Soon, I think."

Angela took the opportunity to get a word in once Corabeth paused to take a breath.

"My, but aren't you an imaginative child. We have not been properly introduced." She held out her hand for Corabeth to shake. "My name is Angela. Who might you be?"

Corabeth took Angela's hand and held it rather than shaking it.

"I'm Corabeth, and I'm a princess. But not the dim cell in the stress kind. I can climb trees and throw rocks, and my dragon can kick anyone's butt!"

"I think, my dear, what you mean to say is that you are not the damsel in distress kind of princess, and I'd wager that you surely are not. But we mustn't say butt. Rock throwing is one thing, a lady must protect herself after all, but you will not be crude. You will speak like a lady. Do you understand?"

"I understand. Are you my mother?" Corabeth asked from behind a yawn, rubbing her eye with her free hand.

"I will care for you; see to your needs, your education, and overall welfare. You will live with Hurd, he is my husband whom you will meet later, and I in this house." She pointed behind her. "We will play games and learn together, you and I. I will hold you when you're scared and mend you when you're ill. I will explain away your questions and teach you to capture your finest dreams. Does this sound to you like a mother?"

"I don't know, maybe," Corabeth said, yawning again.

"Why don't you go inside and pick a bedroom. Any on the second floor will do. I will be in shortly to tuck you in after I've said goodnight to Mr. Gideon."

Corabeth shouted goodbye to me as she ran inside the house. Angela and I just stood there quietly for a moment as the wind picked up through the trees again. As I started to say something, Angela began instead.

"I know that you don't understand tonight's events, Mr. Gideon, but I thank you just the same. This, Corabeth's coming here to stay, is very important to me, to Hurd and me."

"You're right. I don't understand anything about what happened tonight," I told her. "But I promised I'd do for you what you asked. Besides, once I knew what the third item of discussion was about, I couldn't see her go off with that Mr. Trepp."

I swear that Angela flinched at his name.

"I'm sorry, Angela, did I say some –"

"It's nothing, Mr. Gideon, I'm just tired. Thank you, once again." She turned to go into the house. I could see Corabeth wandering from room to room through the upstairs windows.

"Just so you know, Angela, there was some talk tonight at the Gathering. About Corabeth."

"Oh?" She stopped but did not turn back to me.

"It's just, well, they said – some of them said she was evil. That she shouldn't stay here in Timberhaven." Which was a decent enough summary of how that conversation played out, I think.

"Nonsense," Angela nearly spat, facing me. "I've known evil in my life, Mr. Gideon, felt its ramifications quite thoroughly. It is entirely too soon to know who Corabeth will become on that ever elusive *someday* that people talk about. As for now, she is as any beautiful child who comes into this world, made up entirely of slivers of darkness *and* light." She turned back toward the house. "Tell the council of the Gathering that I am quite adept at finding the inner radiance in a soul and coaxing it out. They needn't worry so." She stopped at the door, turning her head only to say, "They should also know, however, that even shadows need a place to play. Goodnight, Mr. Gideon."

And she went inside and closed the door.

I don't know what will come of this strange situation, but as I watch the two of them now, chasing butterflies in Hurd's front yard, I'm glad I helped Angela out. I don't understand even the smallest thing about it, but I'm glad I did it.

Now, enough spying on the neighbors. According to the note from Lady Nicoline that I found on my door, I've got a lunch to get ready for.

Weaving For Dummies, here I come.

* * * * *

I got to Sally's Place a little early, I guess, because I didn't see either Salme or Thegan when I arrived, so I just sat down at the counter.

A young girl with mousey-brown hair asked me if I wanted a menu as she placed a glass of ice water in front of me. Her name tag had a sticker covering it that read *Stop Looking at My Boobs* in neon yellow, blocking the view of her name.

I told her yes, thanks, but that I would be joined by a few others soon.

"Oh, right," she said. "You're the whatsit, the Weevil thing. I know nothing about any of that. Audrey mentioned you might be comin' in today. You know, you're kinda cute for an old guy. I'm Bernie. Hey, Audrey! Front counter!" she yelled to Audrey who was entering from the street at the door behind me. She turned her focus to me again. "I gotta smoke. Audrey will take your order."

As . . . enchanting as Bernie was, I was actually glad to chat with Audrey for a second. I was pretty surprised she held down a job, actually, what with all the running around town that she does.

"Bernadette!" Audrey yelled after her coworker while contending with a very perturbed-looking elderly woman who had followed Audrey in and appeared to be berating her in Russian. I couldn't help but overhear the end of their conversation.

"It's all okay, Nattie, calm down," Audrey said, trying her best to shuffle past the woman. "He's harmless."

"Oh, 'This one does no hurt!' she says to her babushka," the woman huffed, dropping what seemed to me to be her native language for a less fluent but equally flustered English, "Him safe peacock!"

"Nattie," Audrey stifled a smile. "I'm not sure what you're trying to call him, but I'm fine, see?" She did a quick spin around. "I was just having a conversation."

"I no let bad thing happen!" the little wisp of a woman said defiantly. "Spirits tell warning in cards. Tell for Audrey too!"

"Hey, Mr. Gideon!" Audrey said, clearly using taking my order as an excuse to leave the conversation with the Russian woman. "Are you waiting for Lady Nicoline and the others? They usually sit at the back table. Follow this way!"

"I didn't get you into trouble, did I?" I asked as we made our way to the table. "Is that woman the owner?"

"What? Oh, no! No, Natalia is just, well, she's like a mother hen, just peck-peck-pecking around, worried that the sky is falling," she said. "You're not the man we were talking about. It's a gypsy thing. I had a dream a while back and made the mistake of telling her about it. She consulted her cards and bam! Now, well, you saw. Sorry about that. She means well. She's typically very nice. Well, that's not entirely true. It's just, I'm like a granddaughter to her so, it's a fierce mama thing and – oh, ya know what? Just forget this, forget all about it. Hi. How are you? I heard about the Gathering! Things went well?" She seemed very preoccupied. More so than usual. She was fidgety and kept looking up quickly to the diner's entrance whenever someone came in.

We made some small talk, but she soon left to tend to some other diners. Eventually, my lunch mates showed up.

This time, Salme was dressed in a dark blue dress. Made, or so it appeared at any rate, for riding horses. Only a few of the other diner patrons gave her a second glance. Hell, even I'm writing about her like she isn't really a he, even though I met and talked with him instead of her. The things you get used to . . .

Thegan was with her, though he wouldn't meet my eyes at first, just giving me a gruff "Hi" as a greeting.

Salme asked if I'd brought my tape recorder. I said I had. She told me to turn it on and to once again transcribe our conversation, so, here goes:

"Is it on? Recording?" she asked.

"It is. Okay, I – oh, I waited to order until –"

"No, thank you. I apologize but I won't be staying for lunch." Salme said, looking at her watch.

"I'm – sorry, but I thought that you were going to give me a crash course in weaving."

"Thegan will walk you through most of it on your way to the Parson's," Salme explained. "I just, I'm sorry, but I mixed my days up and overbooked. We can certainly get together another time for your questions, but I'm afraid that I must hurry off today. I'll just cover a few things quickly and then leave you in Thegan's capable hands."

"I, uh, okay," I stammered. I'm beginning to hate listening to myself on tape.

"First thing: your tape recorder. Brilliant move on your part, having it handy at the Gathering. I in no way wish to cast doubts on the capability of your memory so far as it lends itself to your writing. But as you wander the streets of Timberhaven, getting to know it, getting the feel of it, you will be bombarded by information. Though you'll still have to write it all down, you'll find that recording things will help you focus your writing for your role as Weaver."

"So, a Weaver writes?" I asked.

"A Weaver creates. Sometimes they do so with words, sometimes images. Sometimes music and song. Even dance. It varies by the Weaver. In your case, it's words." She smiled.

"Okay, easy enough. So what do I write?"

"It will come to you. That leads us to the second thing: wandering the city. Mr. Gideon, it is of the utmost importance that you know Timberhaven. You are not from here, so you will have to court her if you ever wish to know her secrets. Her soul. Yes, cities have souls, just like you and I. They breathe. Their pulses race. They are capable of knowing great joy and wondrous pain. Walk Timberhaven's streets. See her sights, smell her scents. Get a feel for your neighbors."

"So, I wander around and I write what I see? That's it?" Seems like a pretty easy gig. Patty will hate the delay in my book, but it doesn't matter. Not to sound cliché, but I can still feel something pulling me along this path.

"You write what you feel, too, not just what you see. A Weaver lets their creativity ensnare all who reside in their city. That creativity brings strength to the weak and picks up any who fall."

"I still don't understand. No disrespect, but it sounds kind of...New Agey." I honestly wasn't being a smart ass, I just don't get it.

Salme smiled. "It's because I am not explaining well, that's all. But I must leave you now. Thegan will take you to Parson Leets. He will explain much better than I have." She got up and gathered her things. "Come see me this weekend and we'll continue our talk. But remember what I said. Tape things, but still record them on paper. Wander. Explore. You'll be fine."

And she left me there with Thegan, who promptly excused himself to the bathroom. I'm waiting for him outside of Sally's now, listening to my tape and writing everything down. I'm starting to feel pretty stupid, doing everything Salme says without getting any real answers.

Maybe this Parson Leets will be more open and spare me any more riddles.

*   *   *   *   *

June 24, 2010

The strange humming – Dorthea, I guess – woke me up again. Turns out the "only on Thursdays" bit might be true after all. She seemed to be louder this time. Either that or I'm just better adjusted to having gone mad.

It's morning. I'm not sure what time, as I'm writing this on the back porch, listening to the woods behind the house. Lots of life in those trees. I've seen three squirrels so far and what I think was a fox. I've never seen a fox before. Not in real life.

Remember reading *Choose Your Own Adventure* books when we were little? Most kids, when faced with a choice, would keep their finger on that page and then flip ahead in the story to see where each choice led before charging forward.

I was never that kid.

For me, it was all or nothin'. Once I decided to look for lost Amazonian gold by walking along the muddied jungle trail, in lieu of climbing the wind-worn cliffs, it was a done deal.

Timberhaven is quickly becoming my real life Amazon treasure hunt.

I'm making choices that lead me deeper into the drama of this small town, into its tale, and I can't even say why. That's not true, I suppose. I'm a writer, after all. Writers go where the story takes them.

*   *   *   *   *

Back inside now, ready to start playing the tape back.

When Thegan came out of Sally's Place, he was all business.

"A Weaver, you understand, is the backbone of a city's defense," he began as we started to stroll. "He or she must maintain a certain level of readiness at all times, night or day."

"Defense against what? Readiness to write? How does writing a story defend against anything? It doesn't make sense, Thegan."

"I – okay. I'll start again." He wiped his forehead. "When you write, well, why *do* you write?"

"Why do I – I don't know, Thegan, I just do. It's how I earn a living." I was annoyed with riddles.

"Okay, well, um . . ."

"I'm sorry, I just – you have to understand, I'm an educated man. Complex concepts aren't lost on me. But you lot here, man, I gotta tell ya, you can beat around the bush better than anyone I know, and I've worked with movie producers! Now look, I'm sorry. I don't mean to be snippy. You're helping me out here and I didn't mean to get you flustered, so why don't you just take a breath and start one more time."

He took a deep breath. Then he took one more and looked me in the eye.

"You shouldn't have allowed the child to stay here, Mr. Gideon. I'm sorry, but you just shouldn't have done so," he finally said, rubbing a gigantic hand over his stubble-coated face. It was the first time I'd seen him be not cleanly shaved.

"Yeah, I know you were upset by that. Why don't you explain things to me, help me better understand why she shouldn't stay here. And we're friends, Thegan, call me Michael."

"Fine. We don't know everything about the universe we live in, Mr. – I mean Michael, do you believe that?"

That caught me off-guard.

"Uh, well, yeah. Yeah, I guess I believe that, sure."

"If you consider that we don't know everything there is to know, about how the universe works or what all is even out there, would you also be willing to consider that, through study and sacrifice, an individual could make breakthrough after breakthrough before science had a chance to catch up?"

"I don't know, Thegan. Where are you going with this?"

"You're a writer – a fiction writer, which is key. Your clay consists of nothing tangible and yet you can sculpt it into art, into pictures that the mind's eye can see clearly, can mold into a reality all of its own."

"Yes," I said. He had stopped us walking, gently placing his hand on my arm.

"Every human being who can think, who can feel and imagine, can influence reality on some level. Every one. Some only marginally; they don't bother with the talent at an early age and so it will wither away. Others just outgrow the skill, the power, if you will. The day to day labor of their life slowly impedes their ability, so that they can only catch its glimmer while they're caught up in a particularly good episode of their favorite television show."

We started walking again but at a slower pace.

"As Lady Nicoline explained already, every city has a soul. Now, when you take humans and gather them within a city, two things happen. One: people will find like-minded folks to generate a shared reality with. Their entire belief structure – religion, politics, stereotypes, even what kind of food tastes good – will become hardwired into one mass, one network of influence. And Two: a symbiotic relationship develops with these influential networks and their city's soul."

"This is sounding like a sociological exercise more and more, but go ahead," was all I could think to say. I can't say I disagreed with the first part necessarily, but I still wasn't fully on board with cities having souls. People either, for that matter.

"A cycle develops. When the city's soul is shining, it makes it infinitely easier for its people to shine. However, when the city's soul is lost in shadow, so, too, are its people."

"So, what, I write cheerful ditties to keep the populace jacked up on happy vibes?" I asked. I didn't mean to sound so rude, but this was sounding crazy to me.

"In a way, yes. What you don't understand are the effects of the Barrier. What it can do to those of us here in Timberhaven if we're not careful."

"Ah, yeah, tell me about that. It's come up a few times." I wanted to get to some of the weirder topics while he was feeling talkative. Not that people having symbiotic relationships with their town wasn't plenty weird already . . .

"There was a . . . an accident, some years back that resulted in the creation of the Barrier. Now that it's here, it acts like an invisible membrane, capable of great psychic disturbance to the subconscious and conscious mind. And – wait, we're here."

I looked up to find that we'd walked through Timberhaven and come out near the outskirts of town to an apple orchard. There were two men working on what looked to be a paved walkway leading from the street down into the orchard itself.

"We're where?" I asked, kind of amazed.

"Parson Leets' place. I know that all we've discussed sounds outrageous to you and that you probably don't believe me" – I guess he paused to allow me to say that I *did* believe him, but I honestly didn't – "so it's best that you talk to the Parson next. Get his take on things, see how he's been helping until you came along. I'll be waiting here to walk you back."

I made my way down the hill to the gentlemen working as Thegan took a book out of us vest pocket, sat down in the dirt, and read.

I approached as the two men were unloading equipment from the back of a pickup; one, a lumberjack-looking fella, while his friend was a smaller guy who walked with a limp.

"Parson Leets?" I asked.

The lumberjack split his thin beard in half with a great big smile.

"Parson's just a nickname some of the other locals hung me with," he said, walking toward me with his hand out to shake, "Use it if you like, but the name's Jesse. Jesse Leets. You must be Michael, the Weaver. Think you could lend a hand real quick?" he asked, picking up some shovels. "Lots to do today."

I told him sure, and I went to the truck where the other man was unloading.

"I'm Michael, Michael Gideon," I said to the limping man. "What can I unload?"

He shook my hand. "Rick Waller, but everyone calls me Doc on account of my being the vet. Help with the bags of concrete, if you could."

I snagged a bag. Concrete is very heavy, even before you mix it. In hauling the bags I must have inadvertently bumped my tape recorder, turning it off, so I don't have any of the "getting to know you" dialogue the three of us had. It was pleasant enough, as those talks go.

Parson Leets, or Jesse, works construction as his primary source of income. Rick, as I've already mentioned, is a veterinarian. They were building a sidewalk that would run from the road down to the orchard's entrance. They shared with me that a walkway was needed because a Mrs. Ferrera, along with a few other elderly people, couldn't easily make it down to the pavilion area of the orchard. As they explained, I marveled at the orchard itself. It's a thick, beautiful forest, and while I couldn't tell from where we stood at the work spot, it looked like a sign stood at the base of some trees that had grown together in a small clearing by the entrance. Those trees formed what looked like the cupped palm of a hand.

Jesse saw that I was entranced and came over to me. I wanted to make sure that I caught what he said on tape, so I checked my pocket to adjust the recorder. That's when I discovered it had been turned off and I switched it back to record.

"Annie's Orchard. That's what should really get the credit for any help that's come to Timberhaven since the Knight disappeared. All this praise and thanks being laid at my feet, but that's your actual source," he said, staring into the trees.

"That's not the story I was told. I hear you've been very helpful. I don't really understand . . . well, much of anything about any of this. It's weird; the strangest thing I've ever been a part of, but I've got to admit that I'm caught up in the story. Though believing it is something else. I'm not ready to drink the Kool-Aid."

Jesse didn't say anything, only nodded. He seemed very far away. Sarcasm was probably not a good approach, so I thought I'd switch tactics.

"If you don't mind," I asked quietly, feeling as though I had disturbed him at prayer, "who is Annie?"

"Who is Annie. Now that's a story. She was born here in Timberhaven, maiden name of Hedstan, not far from this orchard, actually. Lived about two miles south, as a young kid. Her folks moved the family away when she was around, I dunno, maybe six or seven? Anyhow, she moved back after college, said the world 'out there' was a hard place. That she needed the magic of her childhood to remind her that not everything in this world is ugly."

He bent down and picked up a twig to fiddle with.

"So Annie, she gets back to Timberhaven and she sees, as does everyone who ever goes off into the world and comes back home, that the town of her childhood memories no longer exists. The little shops had all closed up and moved out, and the people, well, the people didn't smile so much anymore; just kept to themselves."

He picked off all the nubs of the twig as he talked and then worked on peeling the bark back.

"Now Annie, she wasn't havin' that. She started up the Old Town Preservation Society so that her Timberhaven couldn't be bulldozed down in the name of progress. She worked day and night, settin' up events to help clean and repair parts of Old Town that were in the severest need of it."

"Sounds like quite a woman," I told him.

"Oh yeah. Only mistake she ever made was fallin' in love with a bum drunk and marryin' him," he said, snapping the twig in half.

"See, Annie, she had a soft spot for damaged things. Felt the need to fix 'em up. Her husband, he was drunk more often than not. Never helped her out with any of the town business. Was heard on more than one occasion making fun of her efforts, actually. Sayin' she should tend to him like she does Timberhaven. He was a vulgar child really, more than a man."

He threw the first piece of twig away.

"About two winters back, Annie's bum of a husband goes on a bender and wrecks her car, totaling it. Now about a week after that, Annie, she needs to make a meeting of some kind or another, and really needs her husband to drive her in his truck. It's a stick shift and Annie never learned to drive one. Still, Annie was doing this for the town. She was *making* that meeting. Story goes she tried to wake her husband to drive her, but – no surprise – he had gotten smashed the night before and was passed out good. So, left with no other choice, she tried to make the trip alone. She lost control and flipped the truck down this embankment here. They found her just outside the orchard."

Jesse threw the other piece of twig.

"I'm, I'm sorry to hear that. She sounds amazing." I couldn't think of anything else to say.

"Her worthless husband, he's done here in Timberhaven. He's gone and he ain't ever coming back. Just the same, Annie's left some good work undone. You may not believe in the things goin' on around you, Michael, and that's fair. It does stretch the imagination a bit. But I believe that good things happen in this world, too, right alongside the bad. Could be optimism is an act of fools in a world where negative's so easy, but someone once told me that if you can't find an example to follow, sometimes you have to be what you believe in. I take that to heart now, and so, every night at seven o'clock, I invite my neighbors to Annie's Orchard to speak on the things that are right in their world. Birth announcements, weddings, soccer game scores or good books. It doesn't matter what, just so long as it's a positive thing, we each stand on the forest's own stage" – he pointed to the trees that had grown together – "and speak our piece."

I was completely lost in Parson Leets' story as I, too, stared into the orchard.

"Now, that's about all I've got to share with you. Not much to tell, really. I'll keep doing what I've been doing here, but I'm not half as smart as Annie was, and I don't have the skills to be a Weaver like you. Get the feel for what you've got to do, Michael, because Timberhaven needs someone to keep her from falling. I've got to get back and help Doc finish up with this walkway here. Thanks for helping with the unloading. Feel free to come out to the orchard and speak some night."

While he went back to his work, I walked down to the orchard before returning to Thegan. As I approached I could see that it *had* been a sign I was seeing from the distance. It was beautifully carved and, as I got closer, I could see what it read:

Annie's Memorial Orchard

Come tell of the beauty in our world.

"Sometimes you have to be what you believe in."

--Annie Hedstan Leets

I walked back up the hill to find Thegan playing washers. At least, that's kind of what it looked like he was doing; only there was no cup or box. He was just pitching the washers into the dirt as he sat there, his book opened in his lap.

"Thegan?" I asked, getting his attention.

He gathered up the washers and placed them in his book as he stood to meet me.

"All done meeting Parson Leets?" He stuck the book inside his ever-present puffy vest.

"Uh, yeah." I was still unraveling my brain from Jesse's story, dealing with the weighted epilogue that reading the orchard's sign had given it and, in turn, losing myself in thoughts and memories of you, Evey. "Hey, why do you guys call him

'Parson' anyway? I was all but expecting to meet some kind of backwoods, fire-and-brimstone preacher when we got here, but he seems more like a woodsman than a churchgoer."

"Correct. Parson Leets is in no way affiliated with any church that I'm aware of. Lady Nicoline gave him the title Parson and the name stuck. Most likely due to the fact that the orchard where he does his good work was at one time church-owned and that he is in all other ways 'tending to the flock' of Timberhaven, if not religiously." Thegan began to lead us back toward town again.

"He's an impressive presence, I'll give him that. And these assemblies of his in the woods, they help out with your – what did you call it – this barrier problem of yours?" I checked that my recorder was recording again. Finding it turned off when I was with Parson Leets had me paranoid that it would happen again and I'd miss some information.

"They do."

"And you've gone to one?"

"Once, yes. I didn't get up and talk, though. Just listened. "

My mind was racing. I felt like too many pieces of this story were being thrown at me, and if I didn't start gathering as many as I could, I might lose the thread of the tale. I was right to worry.

"How's it work? The barrier, I mean."

Thegan stopped and picked up a stick out of the ditch, drawing a circle in the dirt with it.

"You had conceded the point earlier that we, as humans, haven't unlocked all the universe's secrets, yes?" he said.

"Yes. What's the circle about?"

"I'm going to try explaining the Barrier. Only, you've heard the phrase 'you must crawl before you walk'? Well, typically, with the things I'm about to share with you, you'd need many more steps before you should even attempt to walk. You'd need to be conceived, form your brain, eyes, and fingers, be born and *then* crawl – to complete the analogy – but we don't have time for all of that."

He pointed the stick back to his circle, drawing our attention back to the dirt. "Imagine this circle represents all of our reality; past, present, and future. For the sake of argument, I'll pick any point in it, say, here" – he stuck the stick into the dirt at a point in the circle – "to represent that the Big Bang took place, billions and billions of years ago. And then here" – he stuck the stick in at a different point in the circle – "evolution allows for an ameba's ability to go from its primordial home by changing its reality. The ameba transforms; simply growing what it needs to be able to leave."

I found myself so entranced that I sat down as Thegan continued, tapping another section, further along in his circle.

"Here, dinosaurs roamed Earth. A beast mindset reigns, implementing a savagery in our reality's lower level that remains with us to this day."

"Reality's lower level?" I asked, trying not to get lost in Thegan's explanation.

"Yes." He smiled. "Here's where we expand on our circle-in-the-dirt demonstration; provide dimension. Imagine building blocks on the circle; red, yellow, green, and blue building blocks. Now, picture that each evolutionary jump in the circle adds another level of colored blocks. The Big Bang is a level of blue blocks. The ameba's escape, a level of yellow built on top of the blue, and so on and so forth around the circle."

"Okay, blue blocks stacked under yellow blocks, et cetera. That's reality?" I asked.

"You have it!" he said to me, proudly.

"I don't!" I said, frustrated.

"Oh. Let me try further, then. I told you earlier that humans can influence reality, and they can. But they can only work with what was there first; can only take their green blocks and build on the blue and yellow that came before. You cannot wake up one morning and eradicate the savageness in Man by wishing; it's been with us since nearly the beginning. Influencing reality is not the same as controlling it."

"Thegan," I was trying not to completely lose it, "buddy, I need you to stop with the circles and blocks. Just . . . please." I stood up.

"I'm sorry," he said. "I've never been very good with analogies, but I didn't know how else to explain quickly to you what has taken me twenty-odd years of studying to learn."

"Where did you learn this stuff?"

"Oh, I've had many wonderful teachers – brilliant women and men of all walks of life."

I remember thinking that it was too bad nobody ever taught him to teach it to others coherently, but I kept that thought to myself. I was starting to think Thegan was, well, if not crazy, he is very, very weird. I kept that to myself, too.

"Just, okay, how about you take me back to the circle – the one where you were going to explain the Barrier to me? – and finish up so we can call this a day and let me get to my weaving or whatever."

"Yes, splendid!" We returned to the circle.

"But, Thegan, spell it out for me in the simplest of terms. No more little blue and green blocks or dinosaurs."

"Oh." I think I interrupted a return to Jurassic Park, but he got it together. "Okay. The accident I mentioned before, it caused a tear, a, a rip, if you will, in reality, that splits nearly right down the middle of Timberhaven. In an attempt to save all that is, the Barrier was erected. It wasn't a perfect solution, serving as a mere Band-Aid, but it's the best that could be done. Now, as with any bandage that needs changing but isn't tended to properly, the Barrier's begun to fester. Psychic energy is bleeding into our reality from . . . somewhere else, due to the weakened state of the Barrier. The nearer you are to it, the more it pulls your darkest thoughts and feelings to the surface of your mind. If enough citizens succumb to the darkness, Timberhaven will fall. If Timberhaven falls, so falls all of reality."

"Uh-huh," was what I said, because, well, what do you say to something like that? "Well, thanks for giving it to me simply, Thegan. I – can we just take a little break? I need to process."

"No problem, no problem at all, Michael! I'm really enjoying our talk. Truly, so glad to be helping out. You've no idea. And I'm really looking forward to, if you don't mind, once you understand the basic theories, of course, sharing with you my theory that any possible alien encounters that have occurred on

Earth might actually be evolved humans visiting from the future, trying to give us a message!"

I swear if I hadn't taped it I'm not sure that I would have believed this conversation actually took place.

"Thegan, do you really believe all of this? Everything you've told me?"

His smile faltered. "I – why yes, yes I do. Of course. You don't believe it?"

I didn't. How could I? "I believe something is different here in Timberhaven. And I believe that you believe everything you've said. That's all I can give you right now."

We walked quietly for a bit, nearly off of the dirt path we'd taken to the edge of town through the trees. Thegan kept to his thoughts. I started to try and get him talking again when I heard something, a flute of some kind, playing off in the distance.

I stopped Thegan. "Do you hear that? That music?" I asked.

Thegan quickly shook his head as though coming out of a trance. "What? Ah, yes! Maybe that will help. Come on!" He took off through the forest.

It's hard to hear what Thegan's saying on the tape, what with the various sounds of brush and branches that were whipping by me, so I can't transcribe it word for word. From what I remember, he was explaining that what we were hearing sounded like ocarina (I asked him to spell that for me) music, followed up by a small amount of history about the ocarina. Trust me, Evey, you're not missing much in the telling of the tale.

We came to a clearing where we found Lady Nicoline sitting on a stump. Only this time, she was garbed in a white T-shirt and jeans; she wasn't dressed like Lady Nicoline.

"Samuel my friend, good to see you!" Thegan announced.

Samuel, aka Salme, stopped playing his ocarina. "Hello, Thegan." Her – his – voice had even dropped a few octaves. He nodded his head at me. "Weaver."

"We, uh, we heard you playing. Very pretty." God, I sound stupid. Something about Samuel's gaze unnerves me. I always feel like I should be apologizing for something when he's looking at me.

"'Ná déan ach Creideamh'," was his response as he hopped off the stump and stretched.

"Sorry?" I remember thinking that he really doesn't like me much.

"I thought so!" Thegan said. "It sounded familiar. It's an Irish tune, Michael." Thegan then spelled it out for me, thankfully, because I have no idea how I would have written it down here otherwise.

"Where are you fellas at on the lesson front?" Samuel asked as he slipped out of his shoes. He tied the laces together and swung them over his shoulder.

"Oh, well, I was explaining to Michael about the evolution of man's ability to control reality at first, and then we moved on to the . . . you see, I thought if I tried explaining the Barrier –"

Samuel looked up from his shoes at Thegan. "No need. Weaver can do his job just as well without knowing about all that. Why don't you leave him with me, Thegan? Lemme see what I can do with him."

"Well . . ." Thegan looked to me. "I'm not sure that –"

"It's all right. Go on," Samuel interrupted.

"I'll be okay," I told Thegan.

"Okay. I'll wait for you up by the road."

"It's a plan," Samuel said, turning back toward the woods. "I'll have him back to you in a flash."

I followed Samuel as he walked deeper into the woods, stepping over downed trees, through tall grass, and around bushes. There are at least a full ten minutes of nothing but the sound of our forest trudging on the tape. We didn't speak the entire time.

Finally, we came upon a small path and Samuel stopped walking.

"What's your problem?" he asked.

"How do you mean?" And right here, at this point? I'm about to apologize. For what, I have no idea.

"Why are you doing any of this? You don't buy into it. You don't even know what it is you've accepted."

"I'm trying to understand." And again I'm feeling apologetic toward this guy. "I thought you were going to help explain."

"Nah, I'm no teacher. You've drawn the wrong Nicoline for that. Besides, I made no secret of the fact that I didn't want you as Weaver. It should've gone to Cade. His way might've been a messier road, but at least he believed." He started us walking down the path.

"Now hold on a minute –" I started. He was making me mad. Hadn't I said yes to everything? Wasn't I putting off my book, my sole reason for coming here, to help brighten the mood of their entire town?

"Forget it. We're done here. Follow the path up about a half-mile. Thegan should be waiting around the side there." He started to head through the ditch, back into the woods.

"Stop!" I yelled. Like I said, I was pretty pissed. "Come back here. Salme, I –"

He stopped and turned back to me. "Like I said, wrong Nicoline." He turned again to leave.

"Samuel, I meant. Samuel!"

He stopped again. "My but you are a dramatic one. What do you care if I wander off? What do you care if I even particularly like you? With such a small opportunity to get some fishin' in, I'm a man on a mission. But fine, have it your way. I don't want you cryin'. Speak your piece."

I had to calm down a little bit before I could start. I swallowed and took a few deep breaths, trying to convince myself that I wasn't a disappointment to Andy Griffith here.

"I want to be – no – I am Timberhaven's Weaver. I'll tell stories. I may not understand, may not believe that I can help, but I want to. I just need you to point the way."

"Well, it's about time," Samuel said, almost smiling, and took a deep breath. "Thegan's a brilliant mind, but he's trying to teach you too much, too fast. Stick to stories. That's all you need to worry about. A Havener knows this town inside and out blindfolded. You need to, too. Don't rely on that recorder of yours so much. It's catching my words but not the smell of old oak in the forest or the way the sun's dancing off the spider webs over there. Paint the story of Timberhaven in your words, with your talent." He sized up a small tree branch and broke it off, tying some fishing line to the end. "Dark days are comin'. The wolf, well, he may not be at the door yet, but he's definitely got the scent. Up to you to throw him off, buy some time. Keep it all on paper; in your journal, a napkin, whatever you've got handy, but it's got to be paper. A computer is no good to you for this." He stepped back into the woods.

"Is that everything?" I asked after him, standing on the path.

He turned to me, "No. This last bit's real important. You'll have in your journal at some point if you haven't started collecting them already, parts and pieces of the true Timberhaven. All that makes it special. If you do what I'm tellin' you to, you'll be collecting all of the clues a body would need to remind her who she truly is, if the worst happens and she forgets."

And Samuel left.

I walked and found Thegan waiting where Samuel said he would be. He was whistling Samuel's ocarina song.

"Oh, Michael, you're back! That was quick. Come, I'll walk you home."

"Yeah, thanks." Now, I have no idea what made me ask this next question, "Hey, Thegan, what is that song of Samuel's? What's it mean, ná déan ach creideamh?"

He thought it over for a second. "Well, it's Gaelic. Uh, loosely translated into English it would mean . . . belief? Believe. Yes, it means 'do nothing but believe'."

That kept me lost in thought until I got home.

*   *   *   *   *

It's almost five o'clock. Meaning that most of the day has been stolen by Timberhaven. I'm starving. What to eat, what to eat . . .

I'm cooking tonight. Something about the idea just struck me. I don't have much; mac and cheese that I'm crapping up with some onion and broccoli. I'll slice and sauté some of the pears. Think I'll fry some bacon, too.

I found a record player in the Lonely Painting Room (I named it that for the oil painting, a little thing really, hanging all by itself on the wall. A pink carousel with farmyard animals as the seats) while roaming around the house and a box of records in a closet. I put on an album by Betty Davis. I'd never heard of her, but I like the record.

This place feels downright homey now, with the smell of food cooking and music wafting down from upstairs. I opened up the windows in the kitchen and propped both front and back doors open to let the breeze blow through.

It occurs to me that this house's name – Fallenstar Manor – has an origin that is still a mystery to me. Interesting. Considering Dorthea's disembodied humming, this house has a voice and a name . . .

*   *   *   *   *

I had an uninvited guest for dinner.

I had cut my finger while slicing the pears and was cleaning the cut in the bathroom. When I came back to the kitchen, Bernadette, or Bernie, from the diner was reading over my journal.

"Excuse me, what are you doing here?" I asked her. I didn't have the recorder on, so I don't have any of this on tape. I'm going from memory here.

"Door was open," she told me, absently pointing behind her. "And you need a new pen. I was trying to write 'The people here are nut-jobs and are clearly starting to wear off on you. Escape while you can.' in your diary, but the pen's gone dry. Who's Evey?"

"You don't knock?" I took my journal from her, put it away, and went back to my pears.

"Take it easy, Weaver," she said it in a sarcastic, clearly mocking tone. "I just heard the music and, like I said, the door was open. Wouldn't've taken you for a fan of 70s funk."

I explained how I found the record and just wanted some background noise. She started to wander the house, first around the kitchen and then in the living room. I heard the familiar clickety-clack of my typewriter and went in to find her randomly pushing its buttons.

"Look, I'm trying to make my dinner. Was there something you needed?"

"Did you know she was married to Miles Davis?" She acted like I hadn't even asked a question, like I was just an audience member she was impressing. "Probably not, if you don't even know who it is that you're listening to. She was a ballsy chick, man. And to have the kind of influence that she did over someone like Miles Davis? At that point in his career? Pretty damn impressive, claiming a man like him with only her voice. Her body."

She draped herself onto the couch then, and that's when I noticed the short, painted-on black dress she was wearing. Clearly, this business with being Timberhaven's Weaver has me distracted.

"Bernadette, what –"

"It's Bernie. Nobody calls me Bernadette. Well, nobody important. What do you have to drink around here?"

She slowly got up from the couch and slinked over to the cabinet, looking over her shoulder at me. Though I haven't had anything to drink in a week, I still have the bottles around. She grabbed the bourbon.

"Glasses?" she asked, walking back toward me.

"Are you even old enough to drink?" I asked, positioning myself so that the couch was between us like I was a scared little boy. I couldn't help it. Finding oneself in a late-night cable flick all of the sudden is very jarring.

She gave me a wicked little half-grin. "Is *that* really what you want to know? I have a better question for you to ponder: In a dress this tight, are panties really possible?" She walked around the couch, opening the bourbon. "No glasses it is then. My, aren't we heathens." She took a big swig straight from the bottle.

I continued to run away around the couch.

"I'm old enough to be your father," was the argument I half-heartedly raised. I admit that I was beginning to cave to her . . . plan of attack.

But right then she stopped. Her steamy, bedroom eyes quickly faded into a bored look. She took another swig from the bottle.

"S'cool. I'm gonna take the bottle with me, though, all right?" She headed for the door, saying goodbye with the tapping of her high heels on the wood floor. "Great background music choice, by the by," she said, looking back over her shoulder at me again, peeking through her hair like a modern-day Veronica Lake. "Should go great with burnt pears."

Smoke was pouring out of the kitchen. I ran in to take the pan off the stove and when I came back, she was gone.

Odd as this evening has been, do you know what strikes me as the oddest? It just occurred to me that I'm writing all of this down with the pen that she claimed didn't work.

Now I kind of wish she hadn't taken my bourbon . . .

*   *   *   *   *

June 25, 2010

Worst night's sleep ever. I've never tossed and turned so much in my life. That'll teach me to leave the doors open . . .

Lying awake most of the night did give me time to plan out what I want to do today, though, on my trek around Timberhaven. Once I finally quit thinking about . . . burnt pears.

You and I, Evey, along with ~~Mr. Tape Recorder~~ the tape recorder, are going to map out this entire town. Anything that catches our eye goes in the pages.

Just as soon as I find my shoes . . .

Left my house, a.k.a. Fallenstar Manor (mental note to ask
someone, maybe Audrey, about that name today), and now I'm
actually just sitting on my front steps, looking around. Hurd and
Angela's place is the only other house that shares this hill with my
place. It's gorgeous outside this morning. It's been hot lately, but
there's a nice breeze slowly blowing the scattered clouds around
right now.

The forest here does wonders for my creative flow. I went
out the back door of my house to walk the woods there, and for
some reason, a character that I created years ago came to mind.
Inari. She was from a piece I wrote in college entitled *Garden
Exodus*, about a woman who was a slave to maintaining her perfect
rose garden, finally succumbing to the elements in its defense.
Inari was the first time I had to kill a character I loved because the
story demanded it. I haven't thought of her in years.

I feel you here, too, Evey. It's as if you're wandering
around this crazy town with me. It's like you're close. Back like it
was. Like you didn't succumb to . . . like you didn't go. Hate to

admit it, but that grief counselor you arranged for me back home may be on to something.

I came out of the woods onto Hurd's property. He and Angela keep a very neat, orderly yard. Beautiful flowers along a white picket fence, manicured lawn, and even a man-made pond. It's like I walked from the wilderness into a Norman Rockwell painting.

I think I'll head into the Village now, see what's going on there.

*   *   *   *   *

I'm sitting at the pub, the one Thegan and I sat outside of on the first day we met. There's been talk about a bar called Cal's that I have yet to find in Timberhaven, but this pub, merely called The Pub, is an all right place. Gerald, the owner, doesn't really talk much, just brings the food and drink and leaves it at that. As it's almost ten in the morning, the fact that I'm one of a half-dozen in here already tells me that I'm not the only one familiar with Stoley's brand of waking up. I'd join them, typically, but booze still doesn't have the kick for me that it used to. I don't know. Guess I'll stick with the fish and fries that I'm eating.

There are a lot of random pictures in The Pub, mostly of guys standing by their cars, holiday parades, that sort of thing. Basic small town photos.

But two of them caught my interest more than the others. One is hanging by my booth. It's in black and white, dated 1953. A group of men standing outside a cave of some kind. They all look tired. Dirty. No smiles. Evidently, they had been hunting something, because "Crawlshire Hunt" is scrawled in silver marker in the bottom left corner of the picture.

Another picture I noticed, up by the register, is black and white as well. It's of a woman dressed in a swimsuit, staring out over a lake. She looks like a movie star from the thirties. She's very beautiful, but something about her looks . . . haunted. Like the lake had taken something from her.

I overheard Gerald and one of the other old-timers talking. Something about lighting a candle for the window tonight. I tried to listen closer but Gerald caught me and thought I was trying to get his attention. He brought the water pitcher over and refilled my glass.

I'm going to pay the tab and head on.

*   *   *   *   *

The next stop, if I follow the road from my place beyond The Pub, would be Lady Nicoline's place, followed shortly thereafter by Jarboe's Tater Town. Nobody appears to be home at either residence, however, unless you count some of Jarboe's "students" locked up in their cages.

What an eccentric man. I find that I really do like him.

I don't mean to snoop, but there's a picture taped up in his shack, drawn in crayon on notebook paper, of a man, a small child, and maybe a duck? An animal of some kind. The paper is very, very worn. You can still make out arrows, though, that point to each of the picture's stars: Grandpa, Me, Captain Crenshaw.

Jarboe has a family?

*   *   *   *   *

I'm a little ashamed of myself for only seeing Jarboe as one of the eccentric citizens of Timberhaven, stuffed into a role that I placed him in. I wonder where his family lives. Certainly not here in Tater Town. I wonder if they know that he lives like this.

I left Jarboe's and wandered down the street, looking at all of the empty stores along the way. The architecture here in Old Town is primarily from the fifties, lots of gray stonework and straight lines. Straight out of Mayberry, honestly. Small shade trees border the faultlessly kept sidewalks, with stone benches along the way, one every block. I'm currently taking advantage of one of them now.

In a small park across the street from me, there's a little boy sitting in a gazebo, holding a violin case. As I'm watching, he opens the case and removes the violin. He seems to be examining it. Now he's placed the violin under his chin and is drawing the bow across its strings. I've never heard such beautiful music. The music floating over to me from the park doesn't seem like it can possibly be coming from him, yet it is. He can't be more than eight or nine.

I've got to get this on tape.

* * * * *

What a small world. I'm just going to transcribe what I taped, before getting back to the tour.

You can only hear a hint of the music. I should have gotten closer. I didn't recognize the piece, but tears were welling up in my eyes at its beauty. Suddenly, a voice that I *did* recognize plays over the tape.

"Michael? You okay?"

"What?" I had turned, breaking the music's spell, to see Rick Waller, a.k.a. Doc, coming out of the feed store behind me, a large bag in tow.

"I asked if you were okay." He put his bag of feed down and sat next to me on the bench.

"Oh, yes, Rick, I'm fine. Just admiring the music. Very moving."

"Yeah, this one's new. He's been polishing it up all morning."

"Is he your boy?"

"Yes, sir. That's Christopher Philip. His momma and I couldn't pick between either for a first name, so he got landed with both. Most folks call him C.P. though, so I guess neither of us won out."

"And, you're telling me he wrote this piece?" I was blown away.

"Well, I wouldn't say wrote. He draws the songs out, more like. He keeps at it with a piece until he decides that it's done and then moves on to the next song. We've got tape after tape at home."

"What is he, ten years old?"

"Eight, actually," Rick smiled. "But he'll appreciate you thinking he's older."

Christopher Philip stopped playing just then and made his way over to his dad and me. I couldn't quit being amazed by such raw talent. As he started to cross the street, I yelled out to him,

"That was amazing! How long have you been studying?"

He shook his head a little, seemingly perplexed, first at me and then at Rick.

Then Rick started signing to him, speaking aloud as he did so.

"C.P., this is Mr. Gideon. Put your violin down and shake his hand."

He put the violin down and held out his little hand. I didn't take it at first, skipping a few beats as I tried to process what was happening, but I finally shook his hand.

"N-nice to meet you, C.P. I'm –" I turned my head to Rick. "I'm sorry, he can't hear? Does he understand –" I turned back when Christopher Philip started tapping my arm.

"He can read lips – which get him into all kinds of trouble sometimes," Rick said, directing the last to his son, to which C.P. smiled. "But you've got to look at him when you talk so he can." Rick signed some more, "Go see Nora inside. She's got a present for you, for your song."

C.P. gave a really big grin, waved goodbye to me, and ran inside.

"He is truly amazing," was all I could think to say. "How did he, if you don't mind my asking, how did he lose his hearing?"

"That's just the way he was born."

"I don't understand."

"What, how he can play if he never could hear? No one really knows. Just picked up a guitar when he was five and toyed with it until he wrapped his head around how it worked. Then came the drums. Nowadays he's all about the violin, though. Just as like, he'll have moved on to the piano or something else by week's end. Boy's got the attention span of a butterfly in a windstorm."

He got up and grabbed his bag of feed.

"I've got some pups that are looking to get some of this. It was nice chatting with you again, Michael. Come out to the farm and see us, anytime."

"Yeah, good talking to you, too, Rick, and very nice to meet C.P. Until next time."

Of all the wondrous things that I've seen and heard here in Timberhaven, and it's been a wild ride thus far, Christopher Philip may truly be the most magical.

*   *   *   *   *

I left the park and wandered down toward the Village. The buildings get scattered out a bit more the closer you get to the town square and that's when you start to come across the myriad of tents in the Village. Any and all colors of tents. Some are just blankets propped up with shovels while others are eight- and ten-men camping tents, little clotheslines stood up behind them, the day's wash drying in the sun.

A trio of Villagers came walking toward me, heading in the opposite direction. They spoke in cockney accents and were garbed in outlandish robes, reeking of freshly-cut grass. The large man, named Cecil, seemed to constantly bother the smaller man, Alistair, with inane questions while the third of their posse, a slightly unhinged woman named Margaret, simply ran a twisted commentary. The tape picked up some of their conversation as they passed.

"Alistair?" The large man clumped along, holding a teddy bear in one hand and sticking the pinky from his other hand into his ear.

"Yes, Cecil," the smaller man said with an exasperated sigh, clearly tired of questions.

"I don't understand. Why can't Roosevelt be the new Knight? He makes me feel safe at night," Cecil said.

"Because, Cecil, Roosevelt is a stuffed bear. Stuffed bears do not frighten monsters away. They don't frighten anyone away. They are incapable of making anyone feel safe, excepting small children who don't know any better, and you. To suggest to anyone that your toy could protect us would be tantamount to madness."

The woman, who was chewing her hair, stopped long enough to add, "Might as well have me wet socks be the Luminous Knight is what I says, Simple Cecil, you who don't know no better than a wee one." She shoved the end of her hair back into her mouth. "Oy, Alistair," she yelled around her mouthful, "what we gots left in the pouch? Any batt'ries? I wanna throw one at the old clunker car what sits down in the woods yonder."

"Margaret," Alistair replied over his shoulder to her. "No. No, we no longer have anything left to throw. We had some eggs, but you used them all pitching at that cow. So there's tomorrow's breakfast, wasted."

And with that, they were out of range of my tape recorder.

Welcome to Timberhaven. Home to child prodigies and deserters of Wonderland.

*   *   *   *   *

At the edge of the Village, I met up with a group of people, all ages, sitting around a small campfire. A young woman wrapped loosely in a brightly-colored hijab and dressed in blue jeans and sneakers was moving around them, stopping to listen to whoever was speaking every few steps before continuing to circle the group.

"I see a giant serpent," a young man said, concentrating on the fire, "climbing from a pit to attack your monkey."

The circle laughed and applauded at this. The young woman in the hijab noticed me standing there then and waved me over as an elderly woman sitting next to the young man stared into the fire and began her turn at the game they were playing.

As I approached, I began, "I didn't mean to eavesdrop, I –"

The young woman raised her finger to her lips at me, shushing me with a smile.

"I see a –" the older woman faltered for a second, until finally, "rake, held high by a giant to kill your snake."

The circle broke into cheers. Not understanding the rules, I clapped along anyway.

"Very good, very good!" the young woman standing at my side said. "We made it around the entire circle that time." She smiled at the group. "That's enough for today, I think, my sharers of sagas, trumpeters of tales. We can meet again for another round after dinner tonight if you like. Say, in the amphitheater?"

A little boy, after some coaxing from presumably his father, came over and hugged the young woman's legs. "Thank you, Mahin, I had fun!"

"Khahesh mikonam," the young woman, Mahin, said, pulling back her wrap and kneeling down, her long black hair falling loose. "You're very welcome my young friend. Go and enjoy some lunch now. I will see you soon."

At that, the little boy waved and left with the rest of the circle. Mahin gathered a tin cup full of water from a small barrel and doused the fire.

"Looked like a fun game," I said.

"It very much is," she said, making sure the fire was suitably out, "and it is very old."

"What's it called?"

"It has never really had a proper name, so far as I know." She returned the cup to its hook at the side of the water barrel. "But here in Timberhaven, it's known only as Thirteen Words. It is played by storytellers to help exercise the imagination. On a given turn, one must look into the fire and find imagery to defeat the previous player's combatant, using only thirteen words to describe their stroke. No more, no less."

I laughed. "Sounds almost like a game my sister and I played as kids. We didn't use so few words, though." You would have liked this game, Evey.

"That's part of the challenge! It really is better played at night, though. The fire speaks in more open terms, then." Mahin stood before me with her hand outstretched. "I must apologize – where are my manners – my name is Mahin."

"Yes, I've heard your name many times of late." I took her hand and shook it. "All of your new stories kept me from having an audience for bartered figs." I smiled. "I'm Michael."

"Ah, yes, the new Weaver," she said, picking up a small satchel that lay by the barrel. "I would have saved a few of my tales back had I known you'd be beginning! How are you finding the position? Well, I hope."

"Not much to find, yet. I'm still trying to get my footing."

"It's all in the storytelling," she began, "and, trust me when I tell you this as I've traveled the world sharing stories, Timberhaven may well be the richest city in the world so far as stories to tell."

"Oh, of that I'm sure." We began to walk and talk. "And I'm trying my best to keep up with the . . . eccentricities of this place."

"But you're distracted by your own story," Mahin interrupted.

I mulled that over for a bit. "I guess that I am. I'm here to finish writing a novel I've been having trouble with."

"That's not what I mean," Mahin said, smiling, "Creativity, imagination, these are not your problem."

"What do you mean by that?"

"I'm not suggesting that you aren't stuck with your work," she began, "only that – I've told stories my entire life, like my mother before me and her mother before her, and I've learned that everything in life comes down to story. We are each of us, the center of our own piece, while simultaneously bit players in the acts of other people." She sat down on a low rock wall and pulled an apple from her satchel. "I'm a stranger sitting in front of you eating an apple" – she took a bite – "and we're in Timberhaven. Outside of the rich dichotomy inherent in a city continually reinventing itself, here you have a tear in reality as well. One that pulls at every thread of your mind the closer you get to it; dragging your every dark thought, every secret, kicking and screaming into the bright light of day. Like I've said, I am a storyteller too, before anything else, so I get it. How could you not be distracted?"

I sat down on the wall next to Mahin, thinking. She continued munching on her lunch. Finally, I said, "But I don't have a secret."

"You may not be *keeping* a secret," she said, pulling a sandwich bag from her satchel and putting the uneaten half of her apple into it. "But that isn't the same thing as not having one."

*   *   *   *   *

The grass is crunching underfoot as I make my way through some fields just outside of the Village. Everything along the tree line is brownish-green and yellow from having been baked in the heat. I'm taking a breather on an old tree stump. Closing my eyes periodically and letting the sun warm my face while the sounds of the surrounding forest lull me toward a nap worthy of Van Winkle.

I can hear voices coming from just over the hill not thirty feet to my right. Wandering over, I find that it's Brynne, Corabeth, and one other – a red-headed little girl whom I've never seen before but who is the exact replica of Brynne, only in miniature.

The three of them are lying down in the grass and looking up at the clouds as they pass by.

"I think," Corabeth was saying, "that the big one there looks like a castle. See how that other little cloud is circling around it like a moat? Oh, and there comes a catapult from the enemy camp, coming to smash in its walls!" She clapped her little hands together.

"Mommy?" the little red-headed girl said to Brynne.

"Yes, love?"

"Corabeth is weird."

"Reagan DuSayer, you apologize right now! What an unkind thing to say to your new friend!" Brynne said, sitting up as she did so.

Reagan sat up too, mimicking her mother's pose. Corabeth was making battle noises as she watched the clouds float by one another.

"I wasn't meaning it mean!" Reagan said wide-eyed and innocently pulling bits of grass off of Brynne's dress. "She just doesn't like to play right. She doesn't play dolls or house or anything. And she doesn't even know who Dora is!"

"I don't care one whit, young lady. You tell her you're sorry right this instant or we're going home."

"Sorry, Corabeth," Reagan said, staring at her feet.

"What for?" Corabeth asked, getting up off of the ground.

"For calling you weird."

"Oh," Corabeth said, seemingly unclear as to what all of this fuss was about. "Mrs. DuSayer, what does weird mean?"

"Well," Brynne explained, "it means strange. Different. Reagan shouldn't have called you that."

"Really? Mommy Angela says that she's different, too, and that all of the bestest people are. Thank you, Reagan! You're weird, too!"

But Reagan wasn't paying attention to Corabeth; she was looking up the hill at me.

"Mommy, who's that man?" she asked.

Brynne got to her feet, finishing Reagan's job of removing the grass from her dress.

"Michael, hello!"

"Hello, Brynne. Girls. Sorry to interrupt your cloud gazing."

"Not at all." She pulled Reagan in front of her, draping her arms around the child, "Have you met my little one? This is Reagan."

I made my way down the hill to them and held out my hand to Reagan.

"You look exactly like your mom," I told her.

She shook my hand, shyly.

"That's what everyone says. But she's bigger, though," Reagan said to me from behind a curtain of red curls. "And she has boobs."

"Ooookay, then," Brynne said, her face turning as red as her hair. "And with that, I think we'll continue our journey. And you" – she spun Reagan around and picked her up, holding her so that their faces touched nose to nose while Reagan giggled – "I remember a time before you could talk. They were such happy times. People would come from miles around, just to hear little Reagan *not talk*." Reagan continued to giggle.

Then Corabeth came over and took my hand.

"Hello, Mr. Gideon," she said. "We are finding a home for Thayne. I think you should come with us!"

"Oh, Thayne. Yes, that's your dragon, right?" I asked, looking at Brynne with a smile.

"He is!" Corabeth cheered. "He doesn't like staying at my new house, though; there isn't really room for a dragon there. Mommy Angela said that we could find him a new home, someplace close where I can visit him with Reagan, and Mrs. DuSayer said that she would take me to the perfect spot since Mommy Angela couldn't take me."

"We're walking up into the forest, just there," Brynne said, pointing across the field, "it shouldn't be much longer. Care to tag along?"

"Sure, why not," I said as Corabeth dragged me by the hand behind her.

Brynne has a very easygoing sense about her. We talked a bit while the girls ran ahead. (Once again I can't hear anything on the tape over the sounds of walking through the forest. I really need to remember that in the future.) She's a single parent (she seemed happy not to bring up Reagan's father and I left it at that) and alongside playing "Madame Xaxu" out of her tent in the Village, she runs a boutique in New Town. She claims to really have a psychic gift and even says she'll read my cards sometime if I'm game. I think I would like that.

We came out of the trees where, just outside of the forest, an enormous oak tree stood alone at the end of the path, ninety feet high and heralding a steep mountainous hill beyond it. Our little troupe stopped at the base of the tree.

"What do you think, Corabeth? Would Thayne like it here?" Brynne asked, looking up into the gigantic tree's limbs. "It's the tallest tree in all of Timberhaven!"

But Corabeth wasn't paying attention to the old oak. Her eyes were drawn up into the rocky hill above. "Thayne would love it up there!" she yelled.

"Now, Corabeth, Angela said I could take you here, but that was it. Those cliffs are far too high and the gorge beyond entirely too dangerous for us to –"

"But Thayne loves it!" Corabeth pleaded, "He's already heading that way. Don't you see him there?" She pointed up the cliffs as she started toward them.

Foolishly, I actually looked to where she was pointing. She's very convincing, our little Gathering Girl.

"No, Corabeth," Brynne said, grabbing her hand. "It's too dangerous."

"But Mommy!" Reagan began; a new co-pleader in cahoots with her now seemingly not-so-weird friend, "The dragon wants to live up in the rocks!"

"Now don't you start!" Brynne said to her daughter while bringing Corabeth back to the oak tree. "This is where I told Angela we would be, girls. This is where today's adventure ends. You'll just have to tell Thayne to stay put in the tree, Corabeth because that's as far as we go."

Amidst a chorus of unhappy sighs and crocodile tears, the girls finally relented to the unyielding Brynne and examined the tree. As the only other adult around, I tried to help out a little.

"Have you girls ever heard of a Dragon King?" They both shook their heads that they hadn't, but Corabeth especially seemed interested. "A Dragon King, some say, is what all dragons everywhere want to be. They spend their entire lives questing for the right to be a Dragon King. It's not easy, you know. Very few dragons achieve it. They have to be tough. They have to be brave. They have to be smart. And one of the very last things they must do? They've got to find a suitable tree to make into their throne." I had enthralled the girls, Brynne too, it seemed, but I had to finish the spell. "Now I don't know about you, but this tree here, this old oak? It looks pretty amazing to me. Certainly the most powerful tree in all of Timberhaven, so far as I can tell. Don't you think Thayne could be a Dragon King in a tree throne like this?"

"Well," Reagan looked up into the tree, "it *is* very tall."

But Corabeth was looking at me.

"Thayne's never heard of Dragon Kings. He says maybe you're making it up so he'll live in your old tree instead of the rocks above the chasm, where he wants."

"I thought you said Thayne was already up on the rocks," Brynne said with a smile. "How can he have heard Michael's story?"

"I told him in my head what you were saying." Corabeth explained, "But I think you wouldn't lie to me, Mr. Gideon because you are my friend like Reagan is my friend. So I told Thayne he should give the tree a try at least. Dragon Kings sound very different! I'm ready to go back to your house now, Reagan, so we can play some more. But is it okay if we have some of that butter peanut and jellies first?"

And with that, we said our goodbyes. The girls headed back to town as I stayed and transcribed our adventure, seated beneath the newly-acquired residence of Thayne, would-be King of Dragons.

*　　*　　*　　*　　*

I know that I'm supposed to focus on Old Town in my study of Timberhaven, but I wanted to check out Brynne's boutique. I've wandered up into Timberhaven proper, or New Town, as most of the Village refers to it.

I'm sitting on a bench, just as I was this afternoon when I ran into Doc and met C.P., but it doesn't feel like I'm even in the same town. Roughly twenty feet across that invisible threshold dividing Old and New and it's like I'm Dorothy walking out the front door of her tornado-tossed farmhouse into a Technicolor world.

My cell has full bars (I've had thirty-seven missed calls, twenty-eight text messages, and thirteen voicemails, almost all of which are probably from Patty. I'll check them in a little bit.), I have internet access, and I'm currently looking at both a Starbucks and a McDonalds.

I'm watching a crew finish work on a billboard that reads, "Reelect Mayor John Whistleford" above a picture of what appears to be a gleaming-toothed game show host. Underneath his picture, it reads, "Your Champion of Growth". It's the third time I've seen signage about this guy, counting a yard sign and a pin on a lady's shirt I saw as she walked by. She thought I was looking at her shirt I guess because she smiled and proudly told me what name brand it was. (I've already forgotten what name brand she said.)

I am starting to see why Annie Leets was unhappy with the changes to Timberhaven. New Town has none of the feeling, none of the soul, I guess, of Old Town.

There's no magic here.

*　　*　　*　　*　　*

I found Brynne's boutique, called Connla's Well, and looked in the window. It's a typical boutique, really, but with Brynne's flavor; lots of Celtic jewelry, mystical knick-knacks, tchotchkes, and the like.

Across from Connla's Well, though, is another storefront that caught my eye. The window read,

The Daily Scroll

Timberhaven's newspaper since 1939

James L. Mortimer VII, Publisher

I went inside to scope it out a little.

Just inside the door was a desk that at the time was sitting unattended. There was only a little green plant of some kind; some folders and a nameplate sitting on it that read *Vanity Dupree*.

Just as I was inspecting the front office, a tall, thin man, who looked to be in his forties, came to the front counter from the back.

"Vanity – oh, that's right, you're not here. I'll need to . . ." and he turned back around from where he had come, without looking my direction at all, still talking to himself, or Vanity, as it were.

"Excuse me. Hello?" I called after him.

"Much too busy, much too busy! Come back on Monday. Yes, Monday would be better!" He yelled from the back.

"I didn't mean to bother you! Just checking out your establishment!" I yelled back to him.

"Simply can't talk now," he yelled again, seemingly from further away. "Vanity's gone to have her baby and we are out of coffee. The new batch of ink is magenta instead of black, and I think I may be passing a kidney stone but . . ." is everything I caught until he had wandered too far away to understand.

"Oh, okay!" I felt stupid, talking to an empty door behind a counter, so I stopped yelling. On the counter lay some of last week's *Daily Scroll*. The headline read, "Town Officials Come Up Empty". The article was about Timberhaven officials not being able to get around the legislation protecting the local old-time theater. It seems they planned to tear it down to build a parking lot. Beneath that was another article, a note from the publisher, James L. Mortimer VII, which read, *With an apparent appetite for lemon sorbet, Janssen, our beloved sourgum brush, had escaped its kennel and wreaked havoc upon Yolen's dessert cart, causing a dark cloud to descend over the closing ceremony of Leaping Day for those of us at The Daily Scroll.*

I put a dollar on the counter (it felt strange, paying for something with cash besides figs at the grocery store) and kept the copy.

I then saw my way out of The Daily Scroll.

*   *   *   *   *

I'm back at home now, sitting in my living room.

I listened to and read my messages upon leaving The Daily Scroll, only to find that I was right. They were all Patty's.

They ranged from, "Mikey, where are you? How's *Chaos Fair* coming?" to "Gideon, dammit, why don't you pick up? Are you drunk already? Pages, man, pages!"

On and on like that, with progressive frustration on his part it seemed, until, "Okay, I'm officially freaking out. We need that book, my man. Pronto. I'm coming to find you. Where was it you were staying? Some Podunk town. Toledo? Tulsa? No. Dammit! Answer your phone!"

And then he started texting:

"Found your travel plans. Timberhaven. How did you find that dump?"

"En route."

"I'm having to take a bus there since there are no rental cars available. You damn well better have pages to show me!"

And the latest came as I started walking back to Fallenstar Manor:

"Some little shit on this bus pointed out to his mom that I was fat and sweaty. I hope you have a hangover so I can torment you with a hammer."

"E.T.A. thirty minutes."

So now I'm waiting for Patty to show up, fairly certain that what little work on the book I've actually accomplished isn't going to be enough to keep him from chasing me with a hammer, whether he had found me hungover or not.

* * * * *

June 27, 2010

It's been a long weekend, Evey. I'm on the front porch and trying to write this before Patty wakes up. His being here has been entirely too distracting, both from the work on my book and, though I'm still not concrete on the details, from my duties as Weaver.

Patty was in a terrible mood once he finally got here Friday, ranting about being so far in the sticks and away from any recognizable civilization. He dropped his bags; two suitcases and a duffle, along with his Peruvian laptop case that he always keeps within reach. It's hand-stitched leather and he is very proud of it, happy to share how much it had cost him to anyone who will listen.

Pulling a handkerchief from his pocket, he mopped his brow.

"You found me," I said, making a mental note of how much weight Patty had put on since I'd seen him last. He has always been a social creature and highly susceptible to the pleasures of food and drink that come from living the nightlife.

"I assure you," he said, taking on a haughty, aristocratic Englishman tenor, "had you the grace God gives freshly-snipped geldings, you would have simply faxed me the new pages and spared me this country living." He said "country" like he was stepping in something. "But no matter, I'm here now. Spare me a smoke and oh, I don't know, a brandy?"

"Sorry, Patty, I'm out." I made my way to the kitchen while he collapsed dramatically on the couch. "I can offer you a pear, though."

"A pear? What have they done to you here? Fine, I can almost believe that you are out of smokes, but Michael Gideon is never without suitable spirits. If you don't want to share your bourbon, I'll gladly sip on some, eh, what's the local flavor here?"

I stopped and looked out of the kitchen window. How was I supposed to explain why I wasn't drinking anymore?

"Again, apologies Patty. My work had me stuck, and, well, I'd like to try writing this book dry."

Patty exploded with laughter.

"You? Not drinking?" He glanced around the living room. "I've stumbled into one of those reality shows, haven't I? At some point, you'll be covered in chocolate sauce while some well-endowed, bikini-clad Midwestern girl flings playing cards at you in an effort to stick the Queen. Where is the camera crew?"

That brought me back into the living room. "What on Earth are you talking about? I just want to focus on my work. I thought you of all people would appreciate that."

Patty wiped tears from his eyes, "You're serious! You— Michael, just how worried should I be? I don't hear from you for a week or more, you were already behind schedule when you left. You've claims of sobriety. What is going on with you?"

I desperately wanted to get away from the conversation. Patty, who has flown to countless cities in order to come collect my wrecked body after another of my book tour benders, would never believe that I had just stopped drinking. He'd dig for a reason, and I don't even know the reason. Besides, I wasn't ready to share the magic of Timberhaven with anyone from my outside world yet, Evey. It's like when you've put a lot of thought and effort into working a puzzle and somebody else comes along, maybe to take over, placing the last few pieces without you.

"Like I said," I replied, heading toward the stairs, "I want to try this book without any booze. Just to see what happens. I'm gonna run upstairs and take a quick shower, okay? Then I'll take you out for something to eat and some drinks, and we'll discuss my book."

I headed up before he really had a chance to answer.

It was a very short shower, though.

Had I had my head on better, or been thinking straight at all, I would have remembered that Patty is easily bored. With little in Fallenstar Manor to suitably distract him, he would have examined the ingredients label on a can of Spaghetti-O's to get by while I showered.

As it turned out, he had something much more interesting to read.

I jumped out of the shower as soon as the idea dawned on me, wrapped myself in a towel, and ran dripping wet downstairs.

I knew that keeping my activities in Timberhaven a secret from my outside world was no longer an option as I slid into the living room and saw Patty sitting on the couch.

Reading my journal.

"This is . . . interesting," Patty said as he thumbed through its pages. "Is this why you're running behind on the book? You've started a new project of, dare I say, simplistic daydreams? Michael, you know as well as I that fantasy is quite difficult to sell in today's market. This tear in reality that keeps getting mentioned, for instance."

I felt foolish, a grown man standing there wet, wrapped in but a towel and having my diary critiqued and found wanting. Simplistic daydreams?

"And I know the doc said to talk," he used air quotes, "to Evey – look, a sibling's death is hard, I'm sure. I knew you were more wrecked than you were letting on. She was your sister for Christ's sake and –"

"Patty, it's not meant for—stop reading that!" I walked over to take back my property. "You're the second person who has nosed through this. I'm – it's merely an exercise. To loosen things up, get my juices flowing." I grabbed my journal from him, causing his ink pen to fall to the floor.

"Did you write in my journal?" I asked, quite agitated, flipping through some pages to check.

"I certainly tried to edit, but my pen seems to have run dry," he said, running the pen over the back of his hand. A dark red line appeared. "That's strange. But then why wouldn't—no matter." He wiped his hand off on the couch as he looked back to me. "At any rate, I simply can't have any client of mine sending pages out into the world in such a state."

"As I said, it's only a writing exercise. And Evey . . . I'm working through all of that. I'm still working on the book for you, though." I started to head back upstairs.

"That's quite preferable, do you not agree? Stick to horror, Michael. Served you very well, has the darkness and the dead. When people see the name Michael Gideon above the title, they expect there to be monsters. Now hurry along and finish cleaning up. I could simply murder a scotch!"

It was early evening when I came back down to find that Patty had changed into a suit.

"Beatnik hippies or no, I'll dazzle the locals with my high society fashion sense," he told me, straightening his tie. "What's the name of where we'll be dining?"

"The Pub," I said, shaking my head. I knew where Patty would take this.

Patty looked puzzled. "The Pub? Nothing more? My, I certainly can't give them any points for originality. Does it sit next to The Empty Lot? Across the street from The Place That Sells Stuff?"

"Patty," I told him, tying my shoes. "Timberhaven just might surprise you."

He was still laughing at his own wit as we walked out the door. "Do they refer to whiskey as firewater? No, wait, that's more Native American than boring."

"That's enough, Patty. I've made some friends here. Don't embarrass me. Show some class."

He finally stopped laughing just as we got to The Pub. As it was a Friday night, it was much busier than it had been the last time I was there. There was a trio – two ladies dressed laid-back casual in T-shirts and jeans and a guy in a kilt, playing a bluesy rock tune in the corner, surrounded by the ex-hippie crowd who had commandeered every chair in the joint to better facilitate their listening pleasure. Gone were the little old men who played checkers over ham sandwiches and glasses of beer. In their place was a score of early twenty-somethings swarming the bar in nearly every available standing room, sweating together in a shared fantasy of what the Night can bring given suitable liquid encouragement and appropriate bendiness.

I preferred the checkers.

How'd I get so old, Evey?

"First round's on me!" Patty said, making his way to the bar.

I found a table for us and sat down, only to be surprised as to who was at the next table.

"Audrey?"

Audrey turned around. It was a shock to see her done up in actual makeup and not see any paint or charcoal smudges. Her hair was dishwater blonde this time, with two thin black braids framing her face. A young woman with dark skin sitting next to her turned around also, flashing stunningly beautiful eyes.

"Michael? Hello!" Audrey seemed relieved to stop talking to the gentleman, who was noticeably older than her, sitting across from her, and she stood up to face me. "How are you? Oh, I'm sorry this is Nichole," she said, pointing to the girl next to her. "And this is, I'm sorry, I've forgotten your name."

"Hudson," said the man sitting across from Audrey. He finished his beer with a swig. "Another round, ladies?"

Nichole said yes while Audrey said no. "Let me just chat with my friend for a minute and I'll be right back," Audrey explained.

"*I'll* go up with you," Nichole told Hudson. They headed to the bar.

"I don't mean to interrupt your evening, Audrey. I was just surprised to see you here."

"Not at all. It's nice to see a friendly face. I'm not—this really isn't my scene. I was dragged out tonight to 'have a good time' by Nichole and Bernie. Bernie's over there at the bar with Hudson's friend, Mitchell. They just hit town, evidently. We met them outside the bar by their motorcycles."

Hudson is a large man with a stereotypical 'biker' look. His head of black hair is graying in a salt-and-peppered approach to distinguished, which is why I'm writing about him as looking noticeably older than Audrey. I found myself looking at Hudson's massive boots and wondering if they had ever met the face of any unfortunate enough to anger him.

Mitchell, on the other hand, was in his mid-twenties at the oldest. With his pierced ears, dark hair, and scattered tattoos, he looked to be a gypsy pirate. Whatever he was whispering to Bernie, who was dressed to kill just as she was that night in Fallenstar Manor, she was eating up.

"He caught her with magic," Audrey said, also looking to the couple.

"Magic?" The word seemed dull on my tongue. Like a smooth stone loose in my mouth.

"Oh yes. It was actually Hudson that drew Bernie to the pair. She's typically pulled toward older men, you see. But, as we walked over, Mitchell got up off of his motorcycle and produced a single tulip from out of nowhere and held it to her. 'What is your name?' he asked her. Well, she told him, of course, to which he smiled and his kind eyes, they really are so nice, they sort of twinkled. 'Bernie is your Day name,' he said, and I'll never forget what happened next! He kind of, well, he flipped the flower and it was a Queen of Diamonds! And then he said, 'This is the Night,' and flipped the card again and it was a Queen of Spades! And he said, 'Why don't we share some spirits while I discover your true name?' and we came in here. It was magic!"

"That's not exactly what I said," Mitchell had seemingly appeared in front of us, Bernie wrapped around him like a purring kitten discovering catnip. "But I'm pleased you so enjoyed my magic, Audrey." He smiled at her.

"Oh, I really did." She smiled back at him.

"So," Mitchell said, turning to me. "Michael Gideon. Fancy meeting you here. I'm Mitchell." He held out his hand and I shook it, "Mitchell Fairfax. Destiny's a funny thing, don't you agree?"

And a strange kid talking to me like he knew me wasn't even the most bizarre thing to go down in The Pub, Evey, let alone the rest of the evening. The night only got weirder from there.

"I, uh, excuse me?" I noticed that Mitchell had a tattoo of a raven, bordered with the words Pupil of Poe, above his wrist as I ended our handshake.

"Oh don't mind Michael," Bernie said, staring at me from behind Mitchell as she nibbled her way under his arm and around to his chest. "He doesn't much care for good times." She bent back toward me, looking at me upside-down while running her hand through Mitchell's hair.

Mitchell pulled away from her, grabbed a chair from a nearby table, spun and straddled it in one, very fluid motion; sitting in front of me before Bernie had even finished gasping.

"I'm sure that's not true." He grinned. "I can tell a kindred spirit when I meet one. What do you say, Michael? Have a drink with me while we tell each other lies dressed as tales."

Audrey grabbed Bernie and guided her over to their table just as Bernie was about to loosen her whiskey-soaked tongue in what I'm sure was going to be a venomous diatribe aimed at me, based on the look I was getting from her.

"You don't mind, do you, Bernie?" Mitchell asked, taking her hand in his. "Just give me a few minutes to compare notes with our friend here, and I promise you, we'll still have our party."

"Whatever. Think I'll just go join your buddy. Maybe *he'll* want to get laid." Bernie stood up and slowly stumbled her way to the bar toward Hudson and Nichole. Nichole gave her a look that suggested she didn't really want to share.

Mitchell smirked. "Apologies, Michael, for the drama. I seem to attract it." He lit up a cigarette, offered me one and put the pack back into his shirt pocket when I declined. "So, where were we?"

Something about Mitchell annoyed me on the first impression. I can't really say what it was for sure, but it was there. Maybe it's that he's young and cocky, incredibly self-assured. Maybe it's because he can still drink and party like I used to. I don't know. But I didn't do a very good job of concealing my being bugged by him.

"Look," I said, "I'm just here for a couple of drinks with my editor and then I plan on going home. So if you could just go back to the horny drunk girl, maybe we could both salvage our evenings."

Mitchell took a drag from his cigarette, smiling. "All right." He turned to Audrey. "Please excuse my interrupting your conversation with Michael here. I didn't mean any harm." He stood up and finished off his cigarette, putting it out in an ashtray on our table. "You might tell him that it's polite to ask permission before he starts recording folks with that tape recorder of his, though."

I felt my pants pocket for my tape recorder sticking out the top. I honestly forgot that I had it recording. It's a force of habit now, what with how quickly events take place in Timberhaven. I never know when something bizarre will happen.

Like what was about to.

"I – look, it's not," I stammered.

"Hey, no worries, brother, I didn't say that I cared; just that it's polite to ask. Didn't mean to be nosy. It's just, I see a bulge under another man's shirt and I figure it for a gun. It's a safe assumption, where I come from. You have a good night. Look, here comes your buddy – sorry, your editor." Mitchell started to walk away as Patty came over with some beers.

And then, everything went crazy all at once.

"Who have we here?" Patty asked, looking first to Mitchell who kept walking by and then to Audrey.

"Oh, yeah," I said. "Patty, this is Audrey Fell, her dad owns my rental place and she's been kind enough to show me around town a bit, introduce me to some locals. Audrey," I turned to look at her, "this is Patty my – Audrey, what's wrong?"

Audrey's eyes were wide, staring at the bar's entrance. I looked over to see Jarboe standing meekly in the doorway, his eyes drawn to an as-of-yet unaware Bernie. The rest of the bar went quiet; like a tavern in an old western flick when the time comes for the white-hatted marshal to call out the black-hatted cattle rustler for a showdown on Main Street.

"Oh, no," Audrey whispered. She started for the bar. As she got to Mitchell, she touched his arm at the elbow and whispered to him. His face fell, looking at the bar, giving him the first *real* expression I think I'd seen on him all night. His cocksure grin had completely disappeared as he whispered back to Audrey, politely pushing their way through the crowd as they tried to get to the bar.

"Hey, what happened to the music?" Bernie giggled, spinning on her barstool, turning from Hudson's broad arm toward the room behind her. Her drunken smile turned to rage once she noticed what the interruption to her good time was.

"Get out of here!" she slurred at Jarboe. "Get the hell out! Nobody wants to smell your stink!"

"But, my girl, I just thought – on tonight, of all nights –" Jarboe started, stumbling over his words.

"Get the hell out you crazy bastard! Go play with the damn rats you live with!" Bernie knocked her barstool over getting off of it, pushing people to get to the door. Hudson grabbed her while shooting Mitchell an "oh now what the hell" glance.

Bernie grabbed a beer bottle from the bar and made to throw it at Jarboe. Her drunken hands fumbled it, though, flinging the beer backward instead of forward, and the bottle flipped haphazardly away. Right toward Audrey's face. I saw it happening in slow motion and took two steps toward Audrey. "Look out!"

I'm not sure *how* what happened next happened. I know I saw the trajectory of the bottle correctly. It was going to peg her right in the face, I know it was. But then, it didn't. It seemingly, I don't know, veered into a wooden support beam that was two feet to Audrey's *right*. She hadn't even needed to turn her face away to avoid the shattered glass. I got to her and asked, dumbfounded, if she was all right, but her attention had seemingly never left Bernie.

Mitchell had gotten to the bar and helped Hudson to hold Bernie back. Neither man seemed to have an easy time of it.

"Bernadette, I wished only to –" Jarboe kept smoothing his dirty jacket as he fumbled his speech.

"Don't call me that! I'm Bernie! Take that stupid milk jug off your head! I hate you!" She was trying to struggle free of Mitchell and Hudson. "Get off me!"

Jarboe took his milk jug crown off of his head and looked sadly at the floor. For the first time since I'd met him, Jarboe didn't look like the Lord of Tater Town.

He looked like a homeless person.

He turned to leave, crown in hand, as the rest of the bar looked on. Bernie just screamed and cried, fighting off those who kept her from attacking Jarboe, until she fell to the ground in a heap.

"I've got to get her home," Audrey said, making her way around a table.

"I don't – Audrey, what the hell was that?" I asked her. I'd meant the magic beer bottle, but she took my question a different way.

"Oh, it's a long story. She doesn't do well around him. Jarboe typically tries to give her space. I don't know what he was thinking tonight." Audrey stopped to think for a second. "Oh, God. Tonight is when it happened. How could I have –" she continued to make her way across the bar to Bernie.

"What? Why doesn't she like Jarboe?"

She stopped once more before going to Bernie and turned to me. "Bernie has a hard time dealing with her family. Jarboe is her grandpa."

My mind flashed on the hand-drawn picture in Jarboe's lean-to. At the *Grandpa, Me, Captain Crenshaw,* that had been scrawled across the top of it by a child's hand.

Bernie continued her drunken outburst at the bar while everyone who wasn't tending to her was busy trying to get the party started again. A slender woman in an apron was cleaning up the broken bottle while the guy in the kilt fired up his bass. I was going out to see to Jarboe when Patty stopped me, pointing a cold mug of beer at my chest while precariously clutching two more in his other hand.

"Hey, hold on, Michael, where are you going? I've just attained for us some of the finest pints that this, The Pub, has to offer." He handed over the beer meant for me, looking into his mugs, "Such as they are." Patty looked around the bar and back up to Bernie. "My, but you lot tend to linger on the dramatic side of things around here. What do you suppose they'll do for an encore?"

"Stay here, Patty," I told him, not taking the offered beer, and I headed outside to find Jarboe.

Jarboe was sitting on a concrete ring around a small fountain just outside of The Pub, his milk jug sat by his side. I made my way over, watching as he fed bread crumbs from his pockets to the fountain's residents, three, oddly-colored fish.

"You okay, Jarboe?" I asked, sitting down next to him.

"What?" He looked up, his eyes puffy. "Oh, Michael! Hello, hello. Have you met the sisters here?" he asked, gesturing to the fish with one hand as he wiped his face with the other. "The twins are Millicent and Mauve. They tend to run the show over their little sister Clara there." He leaned over to me and in a hushed whisper added, "I give Clara the bigger crumbs when her sisters aren't looking."

"Jarboe," I carefully interjected, "are you okay? Things got a little excited in the bar."

Jarboe looked back to the fish. "Oh, I'm fine. No harm done."

Just then, Mitchell came busting through The Pub's front door, swearing loudly with his shirt dripping wet. He finally made his way over to us.

"I tried to talk her down, man, but she's not having any of it. That Audrey chick is gonna take her home. Man, what a crazy bitch," Mitchell said, wringing beer out of his shirt as he sat down at the fountain's edge.

It happened so fast, again, I can't even say for sure how it happened; like the careening beer bottle inside, I just know that it did. One second Mitchell is sitting by me, drying his shirt. The next, he's lying inside the fountain and holding his left ear, with Jarboe standing over him.

"That, sir, is my granddaughter that you are speaking about. In the future, I expect you'll keep a civil tongue so far as her regard is concerned, or I shall box your ears a second time," Jarboe said, looking down at Mitchell. He made his way over to his crown, speaking to the skittish fish, "Forgive the intrusion, ladies. It's very impolite of us to wreck the tranquility of your home." Jarboe placed his milk jug on his head, looking back to Mitchell. "I should think that it won't happen again." Then he turned and smiled at me. "Always a pleasure, Mr. Gideon! Please do stop by Tater Town for another visit very soon!" he said, offering his hand. I took it in a daze, shaking it and accepting his invitation like I was in a foggy, surreal dream.

As Jarboe left, Mitchell just looked up at me, still sitting half-submerged in the fountain.

"The hell was that?!" he said, spitting out water and nursing his ear. "He hit me in the ear!"

I started laughing and I couldn't stop. I helped Mitchell out of the fountain, giggling all the while.

"Shut up, man, it hurt! Who does that?" he asked, taking my offered arm and getting out, now wet from his head to his boots.

"A grandfather, I guess," I offered, still laughing.

Mitchell sat back down, pulling off his boots. He started to smile. "Yeah, suppose I had it comin'." He chuckled. "The old fart's fast, I'll give him that."

As we both started laughing, I decided then that maybe Mitchell wasn't completely unlikeable.

My sides were killing me from all the laughing by the time Patty came out to find me. Mitchell's friend Hudson wasn't long after him.

"Well, gentlemen, it seems like the excitement inside has drawn to a conclusion," Patty said, sitting next to me.

"Where is she?" Mitchell asked Hudson.

"The quiet one, Audrey, took her home. The black girl wanted to stay, but your nutjob manipulated her into leaving too."

As I considered the unlikelihood of Audrey ever being considered quiet, Mitchell countered to Hudson, "Careful what you say about Bernie. Ya never know who might be listening."

To which, Mitchell and I started laughing again.

Once Mitchell had his boots back on, relatively dried, he said, "We've got a little camp set up in the woods just outside of town. Why don't we buy some booze and head out there? You fellas can help us with this." He held up a tiny plastic bag.

"What is it?" Patty asked.

Hudson sighed. "It was *supposed* to be our party favor for the girls." He looked at Mitchell.

"Well, the girls aren't here, are they? Let's just go be men. Ya know, sit by a fire, tell tales, kill and dress a wild boar."

Patty asked to see the bag, inspecting it.

"I'm in," he said.

"Fine." Hudson huffed. "Lemme get the bikes."

"What about you, story man, you looking to go down the rabbit hole?" Mitchell asked me.

I don't know why, but I said sure.

And then, unbelievable as it is, things got even *weirder*.

Timberhaven weird.

Hudson hadn't wanted to walk the motorcycles back to the campsite, which had been Mitchell's suggestion once it was understood that Patty was in no shape to share a ride back.

"Fine, he can ride mine and I'll walk back with Michael," Mitchell told Hudson, digging into his pocket. He pulled out his keys and pitched them to Patty, who promptly dropped them.

Hudson looked at Patty and then back to Mitchell, shaking his head.

"I'm gonna ask a stupid question here, but have you ever ridden?" Hudson asked Patty.

"Well, I mean, *look* at me." Patty sucked in his considerable gut. At least, I think that's what he was doing. "Don't my abs just *scream* motorcycle enthusiast? I'm an avid rock climber and marathon runner too since we're sharing." He picked up the keys. "I'll figure it out."

Hudson simply shrugged at Mitchell as if to say, "Hey, man, it's your bike."

While Mitchell went over and talked Hudson into not leaving Patty behind, I rushed to Patty's side as he attempted to locate his sense of balance on Mitchell's motorcycle.

"You sure you want to do this?" I asked.

"I am the master of the motorways, the king of –" he slipped, sliding too far over one side and catching himself with his outstretched toes while I countered his fall, pulling the bike in the other direction. "It's the absence of suitable pavement that's throwing me," he muttered, climbing back up on the bike. "It has very shoddy roadwork, your adopted town."

"That's just what I was thinking," I told him, an eye roll evident in my tone.

Once Hudson promised not to leave Patty stranded, the two made their way off into the night, very, very slowly. Hudson looked like someone who was trying to walk a very much drunk, overly-curious puppy, one that veered back and forth from tree to tree in strange, clumsy loops.

Once they were gone, our entertainment in watching Patty concluded, Mitchell and I began walking. It was a quiet night. I remember hearing the dull murmur coming from inside the bar, but that outside it was calm. A soft breeze was the only sound you could pinpoint as noise, outside of our footsteps as we made our way through town.

As we crossed onto the pathways of the woods, I noticed that Mitchell was fiddling with his little plastic bag, emptying its contents into a small flask.

"What is that?" I asked.

"This? This, my fellow road writer, is Morpheus Dust," he said, sealing the flask and shaking it up.

"Morpheus Dust? I've never heard of it. What am I getting into here?"

"I'm not surprised you don't know it. This, Michael, is a sacred rite of creation; strong hoodoo. I wouldn't even entertain sharing with you if I didn't think you were worthy," he said, handing me the flask.

"Yeah right." I smiled. "You and Hudson were all set to share it with some teenage girls, so you can take that line on down the road."

"Nah, they were only going to share the Dust by itself. I wouldn't have mixed the flask for them."

As I've noted to you many times now, Evey, I quit thinking about booze not long after coming to Timberhaven, for whatever reason. I can't say why, but I happily unscrewed the top of that flask and took a shot. It tasted like strong tea mixed with whiskey. My chest was engulfed in bladed flames as the liquid made its way down my throat.

Mitchell laughed at my coughing.

"Christ, man! Way to jump in with both feet!" He took the flask back as I doubled over; my hands on my knees, debating on whether vomiting would hurt more than keeping it down.

Once I could remember how to form words, I managed one in particular. "Poison." My voice was so weak I can't even hear myself on the tape recorder.

Mitchell only laughed some more.

"I didn't poison you, Michael. You just took too much. You were supposed to sip it and hold it under your tongue – a fact I would have shared had you not gulped it down! Hudson and your buddy have some back at camp. The plan was to arrive at the same time, but now, if we don't hurry, you'll land long before the rest of us and get lost."

"It might get a little intense," Mitchell said and swigged from the flask. "Just try and wait for me."

Oh no. The tape doesn't seem to be playing back anything after that. It recorded, like before with Mr. Trepp, only this time I don't even hear any forest noise. The recorder didn't pick up any sounds at all.

I even turned up the recorder to full volume to be sure.

Nothing.

Well, okay, I'll fly solo on this one. The next thing I remember, the burning in my chest had subsided a bit. I could breathe again. I looked over to Mitchell who was sitting on the ground holding his knees to his chest. He had his head up, looking into the sky and mumbling over and over, "It's full of stars!"

I glanced around, then, trying to get a feel for where we were. I remember hearing a low hum, like the sound of electricity running through a wire fence or my electric razor getting triggered on while still inside the bathroom drawer. It was coming from the forest around us.

I asked aloud, "What is that sound?"

I saw, from the corner of my eye, what I can only describe as a big, purple inkblot. When I turned my head to find it, it swerved to the left, back to the corner of my eye's vision. I tried to catch it again, only to fail.

"Just so it's clear, you should know that you look stupid when you do that," I heard a voice say.

"What?" I looked around and found a raccoon down by my feet. How I knew it was a raccoon, what with it being night time, I don't really know. But it was.

"I said," the voice came from the raccoon, "that you look stupid when you chase your tail like that. Mostly since you don't have a tail, but I can't say that you would look any less stupid if you did have one."

"But" – I sat down in front of it – "raccoons don't talk."

"Right and you humans don't shit where you live," it retorted.

"What's that you're doin'?" asked another voice from somewhere in the woods, one that I somehow knew came from a mole.

"Playing Redundant False Statements with this guy here," said the raccoon.

"Ooo, I love that game!" came the mole. "Pheasants are great roommates! Squirrels don't walk funny after sex!"

"I was being sarcastic, Quarry. This guy's as inebriated as the day is long," the raccoon told the mole, whose name was Quarry it seemed.

"What's he doing gettin' stoned this close to the Barrier, eh Amble?" returned the mole to the raccoon, whose name, obviously, was Amble. "He crazy?"

"I think maybe I am," I told them both, the talking raccoon and mole.

"Could be you are," Amble told me, eyeing me from head to toe, "but that's not my place to say. A man's business is his own."

Quarry sauntered right up to my feet, as I recall, sniffing my shoes with his mole nose and feeling them all over with his tiny paws.

"That mean we're done playing RFS? Phooey. I always come in at the end of a round," Quarry said, looking up at Amble and me.

"Setting aside that you both can talk," I said, while I mentally acknowledged that Morpheus Dust is a little intense in the same way that the Hindenburg hit a little snafu, "how is it that I can hear you, little guy? You're way down by my feet, after all."

Quarry harrumphed and walked back over to Amble, his nose up in the air.

"That's just how they are on their side, Quarry, don't pay him any attention," Amble said, bending over to pat Quarry on the head. "Listen, mister, this has been fun and all, but we're looking for a guy name of Gideon. We were told to find him here. Ya don't happen to know who I'm talking about, do ya? Young guy, short dark hair–"

"Gassy," added Quarry, jumping back into the conversation.

"Yeah, that's right, gassy. A real burper. Kinda stumbles around from place to place, too."

I didn't know what they meant by gassy and stumbling around, but I said, "I'm Gideon. Michael Gideon." I'm only just realizing as I write this now how stoned I must have been. Details of the episode are slowly coming back to me.

"Uh, yeah," Amble said while Quarry rolled around on his back, laughing, "Not for nothin' fella, but you ain't exactly what's generally considered young by your standards, are ya? I only mention it because, well, you look a little long in the tooth."

"It's funny 'cause it's true!" Quarry laughed, having now rolled over onto his stomach. Amble poked him in the ribs with his foot.

"Hush, Quarry! Sorry. He gets excitable when we're doing business."

"I see. And what business would that be?" I asked the raccoon.

"Oh!" Amble yelped, licking his paws and sorting his facial fur. "We're businessbeasts," he said as he handed me half of a cleaved walnut. Inside the walnut read:

A&Q Collectors

Acquirers of Original Tales,

Unearthed Mysteries and

Lost Causes

"Original Tales? Is that why you're looking for me?" I asked, handing Amble back his walnut.

"Well, no, we're looking for *Gideon*," he annunciated, clearly still not buying that I was who they were looking for. "For another matter. Private business. Privileged client," he said as he stored his "card" in whatever hiding place he'd pulled it from.

"Like I said, my name is Michael Gideon, but if you're sure you aren't looking for me, I'll just be on my way with my friend here."

"Who's that, then? What friend?" Amble asked, peering around me into the darkness.

I looked to where Mitchell had been sitting, looking at the stars. He wasn't there.

"A guy, a man I met tonight. He was sitting there a second ago."

"You were all alone when we saw you," Amble explained. "How high *are* you?"

Just then, what looked to be a thick, sinewy, black length of rope shot by my face. I dropped to the ground to avoid being hit as it shot across into the trees.

"Where did that come from?" Amble asked.

"Amble, something's out there," Quarry said in a hushed, trembled whisper as he pointed through the trees. "Something wicked. I say we forget our Gideon and just give it to this guy."

"But he's not the right Gideon!" Amble whispered back, keeping low to the ground.

The thing that was like a black rope shot past again, making me hit the ground to avoid it. This thing, this thick rope, radiated – I hate to admit this of a . . . rope – but it radiated sickness and wrong.

"I've got to find the people I came with and get out of these woods!" I told the raccoon and the mole. "Where are the camping grounds?"

"Camping grounds?" Quarry said, exasperated. "Where do you think you are?"

As I surveyed my surroundings, aware of the presence of an evil stretch of rope and discussing it with a couple of businessbeasts, I realized that I honestly couldn't say where I was.

"Fine, fine. You don't have to keep at me about it," Amble said while Quarry was pushing him toward me, the black rope thing crashing through the forest around us. "Here, take this."

The raccoon handed me a conch shell.

"What is this?" I asked. In hindsight, Evey, I know it seems strange that I forgot about the black rope long enough to question, albeit limitedly, a raccoon as to why it was handing me a conch shell while his mole partner quivered in fear. Nevertheless . . .

"It's the message for Gideon," Amble said, ducking while covering Quarry. "Which, whether I like it or not, is now you. Mind that nasty rope business you brought with you whenever you leave."

And then they were gone, escaping into the forest.

I sat down, preparing for the rope to attack again, but nothing happened. I looked over the conch shell, carefully examining it for writing of any kind and coming up empty. Finally, I put it to my ear.

"What the hell are you playing at, Gideon?!" came a voice from inside the conch shell; a voice that I recognized from somewhere but couldn't place where. "This was not part of our deal! Get back outside of the Barrier, now!"

Stunned, I dropped the shell. Just then, the black ligament that looked like rope, or vice-versa, came snaking back out of the forest, slowly caressing the ground like a hunting viper. I got up and walked in the direction that I thought the others had gone down on the motorcycles. I wanted to yell for Mitchell but thought I'd wait until I couldn't hear the rope monster sliding around in the grass.

Just so I can understand what I was thinking when I read my journal in the years to come, I get, while I'm writing this, that I was hallucinating on the Morpheus Dust. But it's the most vivid trip I've ever had. The details are amazing. Maybe Mahin's story had been more than a story after all?

Anyway.

As I walked I heard water splashing from somewhere through the bushes ahead of me. I came into a clearing near a lake's edge. Climbing out of the water onto a large, nearby rock on the beach was a young man, a teen by the look of him. His dark skin made the white shorts he was wearing all the brighter.

"What you want here, man?" he asked me, pulling a shirt that read *Coix* over his head.

"I'm lost," I muttered.

"Ain't we all." He climbed down from the rock and made his way over to me. "Lucky for you, I know where you're heading." He walked past me. "Let's go."

With a lack of any other solid direction to follow, I went with Coix back into the woods.

"Be careful out here," I said to him. "There's a snake of some kind." I'd never seen a snake act like that, though.

"S'no snake," Coix said. "Or maybe it is. Things in here are seldom what they seem. Unless they're exactly what they're playing at being."

I let the absurdity of his words go. My mouth was starting to get very dry.

"I can offer neither drink nor drug," Coix said over his shoulder.

"That's okay. Where are we going? I'm Michael – "

"Gideon, yeah. You think I know the path but don't know who it is I'm takin'? We're going back to the outside. Well, *you* are."

I followed quietly for a bit. Coix was very surefooted in the forest. I kept stumbling over tree roots and loose rock.

"Your feet are heavy. There was a man once who said that heavy feet led to nowhere snappy. Good thing, I guess, that I'm leadin' instead of you."

"Are you real?" I remember suddenly questioning everything, thinking that was a sign that I was sobering up, maybe, or about to find the next level of the Morpheus Dust. I was desperately hoping for the former. "Because talking animals came earlier, and I'm pretty sure *they* weren't real. Relatively sure."

Coix stopped walking and turned to face me. His self-assured grin was frustrating, but I couldn't say why. "What is real? Ambition is only quantifiable when compared to a lesser degree. Use your words; you with the heavy feet and dead eyes. What do you see? Feel? Taste, smell or hear? Can you REALly do these things? In your concrete world with your plastic toys. I've taken potbellied pigs parading past pink pavilions. Were we real? The asker holds no sway. It's the question that lacks tact. In a world of free men, agenda is an ugly word. But now the old man's favor is done."

Coix poked me in the forehead, and I came to, lying on the ground near Mitchell where I'd taken the Morpheus Dust hit, covered in sweat and meeting the sun as it rose.

"Mitchell?" I had to fast forward through all of the silence on the tape but there's my groggy voice. I wasn't really expecting my hallucinations to be captured by electronic means, but still. Mitchell began to stir when I said his name.

"Ugh. And I *mean* ugh. I feel like I've just been birthed through a goose's butt."

"What the hell happened? What is that stuff, that Morpheus Dust?" I tried to get up and found that it wasn't as easy as I remembered.

"What do you mean? It's cool. You're fine." He stood up and gave his head a quick shake, still a little wobbly. "Guess we didn't make it back to camp. Let's go get the others. I'm starving."

I kept the Amble and Quarry meet and greet to myself, not seeing the need to bring up talking forest dwellers, but I had to ask about Coix. "Did we hang out with some young guy? A kid, really, some kind of a street poet maybe?"

Mitchell laughed. "No. Not that I remember. Man, you are such a lightweight!"

Mitchell helped me up, and we started walking toward where Patty and Hudson had ridden off to camp. I felt too unsteady, though, and my head was killing me.

"I'm calling this party over. Think I'll just walk back to my place. Tell Patty, huh?"

Mitchell took me by the shoulder. "Okay, brother. You go forth and, well, do whatever it is you do after a night out. How about tonight? You good to go again? I feel bad about knocking you out with the Dust, so drinks are on me." He headed off down the pathway through the woods, not waiting for my reply.

As I headed back to the house my head was swimming with the night's events, with everything I've listed here. There's nothing on the recorder after that – a night of recording nothing tends to wipe the tape, so I walked back in silence wondering who that voice in the conch shell belonged to. Hallucination or not, I know that I recognize it from somewhere.

The walk back was uneventful, as was the rest of last night since I waved off all entreaties to spend the evening drowning in cups. Patty went with them in my stead, touting about the bevy of women that the trio would pick up. He was quite wasted when he returned here at four this morning but wasn't accompanied by the fairer sex.

I spent the evening here, all because of one thing the hallucination that was Coix said to me: Potbellied pigs parading past pink pavilions.

I remembered the phrase once I got back to Fallenstar Manor, and that made me think of the painting in the Lonely Painting Room: a pink carousel with farmyard animal seats. Two of which are pigs. Once I was alone, I ran up to the room and snatched the painting off the wall, investigating it inch by inch. It's painted by an untrained hand which is probably why I dismissed it at a glance before. Well, that and it's a merry-go-round with barn creatures. But then I noticed the house behind the carousel.

It's Fallenstar Manor.

This was freaky enough by itself before I noticed some of the other things in the painting. In the corner is a little old woman, standing behind her fence and pointing at Fallenstar Manor. In the foreground, next to the carousel is a large tree. Its branches were all withering except one strong limb, coated with leaves. That limb also pointed at the house. So I took a closer look. I couldn't figure out what I was missing.

You with the heavy feet and dead eyes.

Then I saw it. The windows. My manor, my home here in Timberhaven, has three bottom windows at the front of the house and three top windows. The manor in the painting has four windows each, top and bottom.

I took the painting and walked around and around the house, over and over. I was obsessed with imagined clues and false leads. What did the extra windows mean? Are there hidden rooms? So I spent the night knocking on walls and checking light fixtures. I pulled at floorboards and moved rugs. By the time Patty got back, I had turned the house upside down, all for nothing.

Exhausted, I went to bed after cleaning up the crock pot that Patty puked in. I gathered up the blankets and threw them on the floor, opting for the sheet instead. As I laid there going over the events of the weekend, meeting Mitchell, the Morpheus Dust, Mahin's story, discovering Jarboe's connection to Bernie, Audrey, and the magic beer bottle, it occurred to me how much I've changed in these past two weeks. I reread this journal sometimes and wonder if I've completely lost my mind. It seems too much to have happened in such a short period.

If I hadn't written it all down . . .

I dreamt of strange tidings once sleep found me. I was at The Pub, eating a turkey sandwich. A very old German shepherd came in the front door and padded over to my table. "Might interest regular readers," it said to me. Then it walked back out the door and into an operating room. Afterwards, Gerald came up to me and said, "Best heed her, she's the owner. That'll be $17.50." And handed me a bill for my sandwich.

And when I woke up, I swore I would never touch Morpheus Dust again as long as I lived.

It's a beautiful morning outside, but I hear Patty bumping around in the bathroom and I need to pick up the house before he starts asking why I tore it up in the first place. Houseguests, who needs 'em?

* * * * *

June 27, 2010

Got everything cleaned before Patty was any the wiser. I sent him off to find some alcohol for the house, a mission he was more than happy to take on. I should have a little time to work things through in my head. About the painting, the hallucinations, hell, Timberhaven in general.

First of all, I believe that it's clearly Angela in the painting, pointing to the house. I tried to run next door and talk to her, but nobody answered when I knocked. I looked back at their house when I got to my yard, though, and saw Corabeth at the circular attic window. Her expression was blank. Not smiling. Not waving. Just an empty stare my way as I left.

Chalk her up as another hit on the list of mysteries here in Timberhaven.

That's not a bad idea . . .

* * * * *

I skimmed back through my journal and pulled any and all weird goings-on collected herein – there are more than a few – in an effort to, I don't know, look for clues. For seemingly random interconnectedness. The tapestry of Timberhaven's secrets, if you will.

It's fitting, I think, what with my being their Weaver.

I'm putting these down in roughly chronological order of appearance. Focus, investigate and discover. That's my plan. Well, that and staying away from Morpheus Dust. Okay:

1. The forests here in town, particularly around my house. They play on my mind a lot while I walk through them, both focusing my ability to write and drudging up work of mine I haven't thought about in years.

2. Audrey Fell. She knows things about everybody in town, it seems. Got to sit her down for an interview. A proper Q & A.

3. Hurd and Angela. Where is Hurd? What was the deal with his all-night dance routine? Is he now hurt somehow, laid up in bed? Why did Angela think I might feel guilty for whatever has happened to him?

4. Things around the manor: the mirror on the wall, the song that I can only hear on Thursdays sung by Dorthea who isn't really there, the pears showing up, the painting, etc.

5. The events, whatever they may have been, on the night of the 18th. Why I don't remember anything that occurred from

three to nine a.m. and why the hell I haven't been myself on the booze front since.

6. The bizarre dreams I've had since I've been in Timberhaven. The insane visions while I'm awake. I'm realizing that a lot of them center on *Chaos Fair,* a novel that I'm having a harder time with than any other of my career. Plus, how the hell does Lady Nicoline know about my dreams and visions?

7. Lady Nicoline in general. The voice of three? Samuel? Salme? <u>Who makes three?</u>

8. The Gathering. Mr. Trepp with his not being recorded on tape thing and just overall creepiness. Weavers. Knights who protect dreams. And Corabeth? I don't even know where to begin with her. A group of adults having a meeting like that at all is beyond anything I've ever dealt with before.

That's enough of a go, I think. If I try to focus on any more from the almost anarchic pool of oddities around Timberhaven, I'll continue not getting anywhere. Now I've got to align the facts, just like if I was writing a nonfiction article. Follow down leads, that sort of thing. Definitely need to sit down with Audrey and probably Thegan, too.

I'm going to solve these eight things. Riddle them out. Maybe those answers will give me the clues to the next batch of mysteries here. It's a path at least.

I haven't been this excited about a story in years.

The difference is I can't just make up things to suit my needs like I can with my fiction work. That's going to take some getting used to, particularly since my imagination is firing like crazy these days. Focus on the things I know; what I can see, touch and feel. That's what I've got to do.

Patty is going to be a problem. His being here is going to hinder my investigation, not to mention my role in Timberhaven's affairs. I've got to get him to head back to New York so he won't distract me. We'll sit down when he gets back and discuss my book. Maybe after he offers some insight, some notes, on what he wants me to do I can get him to hop on a plane. I'd even go back to The Pub for a drink with him after if it will speed him on his way.

Someone's knocking at the door. . .

It's Brynne! I just got asked out by Madame Xaxu herself. She's waiting downstairs while I get cleaned up for, as she puts it, a night on the town.

I'll deal with my houseguest later.

*   *   *   *   *

June 28, 2010

Where to begin. . .

Things started out fantastically with Brynne. I don't remember the last time I enjoyed a Sunday that much. She's an incredible woman. I like her a lot.

God, I sound like some inarticulate kid!

Man, you'd be making fun of me if you were here, Evey.

It was a great time, is all.

With Patty around I've taken to keeping my journal on me almost all the time – my tape recorder, too – so I wouldn't be found wanting in case any Weaver business came up while Brynne and I were out together. And, of course, it did.

We started with an afternoon walk around the Village. She looked beautiful in a simple brown dress and sandals.

"No Reagan today?" I asked as we inspected a stash of homemade garden gnomes that a guy named Clint was selling from his bicycle.

"She's with Anthony. They're watching a documentary on the Andromeda Galaxy that he brought over. It's all Reagan has talked about for the last two days." She examined a gnome made of an old tennis shoe. On top of its head was a pointy hat made from a paper drinking cup, coated in blue paint patterns by what looked to be a fork. "Normally I'd sit with them, but I took the opportunity to have some me time."

"Oh." I sound on the tape as bummed as I felt at the time, which goes far in explaining what I asked next, "Is Anthony your boyfriend?"

Brynne's laughter is a sweet song, even when directed at me. I'm smiling now as I listen to it.

"I'm sorry, I don't mean to laugh – but no, Anthony's not my boyfriend. You know him as Thegan. Anthony's his first name. But way to just come right out and ask me; the upfront approach. I don't often get that," she said, smiling at me.

I felt like my face was going to split in half, I had such a big smile.

"Oh! No, I," – as I tried to recover with a shred of self-confidence – "his name isn't Thegan?" – Brilliant! Misdirection – "I guess I didn't really even stop to consider – though, now that I think about it, I do seem to know a few people by only one name here in Timberhaven!"

"Yep, I've always preferred Anthony, but most around here refer to him as Thegan, too." She turned to Clint. "I'm sorry, but my daughter has my garden quite well-stocked with garden protectors, I'm afraid. At this point, the gnomes outnumber the potatoes two to one."

"What about Jarboe?" I asked as we continued on our way.

"Lord Jarboe, "she corrected me. "Prefers Jarboe. I forget how he came to the name; something from his youth. He won't answer to his birth name anymore, not since Timothy died. But I feel as though we're gossiping now, and I can't stand gossip. Being the center of it more than once, I can tell you, it's not a healthy way to spend one's time."

I remembered looking for figs before the Gathering and hearing from Mrs. Pinley about the beauty of one Madam Xaxu. It was not a tale told from a friendly perspective, but it did remind me . . .

"Ah, yes! You, Madam Xaxu, owe me a reading. I recall you offered me one while we spent an afternoon seeking a home for a destitute dragon. Come, come I must hold you to your honor." I extended my arm to her. Evidently, I'm a dork. Luckily she is, too.

"You are correct, good sir," she said, taking my arm in hers. "I did indeed. But beware," she took on a thick European accent, "for Madam Xaxu speaks only in truths. In her tent your soul will be naked; your secrets, exposed."

"Naked and exposed in a tent with a beautiful woman. Hmmm, I can't really see the downside to that scenario. Lead on!" It's a wonder I've ever known the touch of a woman.

"Oh! Wicked man!" she said, laughing – quite generous of her – and dropping her accent as we ran hand in hand like two high school kids toward her tent in the Village.

The Village was fairly busy. Next to a woman who was walking on her hands while performing *Oliver Twist* (her feet were painted to look like orphans) was a man blowing fire of various colors. Across from them were an elderly painter, a young girl who had built a model of the Alps out of what smelled like manure and some kind of tropical flavored shaved ice, and a middle-aged man who seemed to be in a trance.

"What's he doing?" I'd asked Brynne as we slowed down to maneuver traffic. Say what you will about the Village, but it has been steadily filling with people since I've been here. "That man over there sitting on the giant pillow."

"Oh." Brynne smiled. "That's George. He's 'cavorting with the spirits' again."

"He looks rather stoned."

Brynne laughed. "Yes, I guess he does! He's performing automatic writing. That's what the pad of paper is for, see? He puts himself in a trance and then waits for a spirit to move through him and write a message." She leaned in close to my ear. "It's not real. Don't believe it."

"The psychic is telling me that the man's possession isn't real?" I whispered back.

"Oh, you just wait! Mocking the psychic, I swear." Brynne smiled, "I don't mean that it's not real, just that what he's doing is not a mystical thing, but a subconscious one. More often than not he gets messages from dead pirates or aliens from deep space, but it's really just his inner voice firing synapses while he's catatonic, disposing of unneeded material."

I flashed on what Mahin had said earlier, about my having secrets I didn't know about, but I shook my head and moved past it, "Sounds like some of my books. How do you know so much about automatic writing?"

"Occupational hazard. When you grow up with a gift, you discover all kinds of other information while trying to understand it. Speaking of which, here we are."

Brynne's tent is huge. Like something out of an old black and white movie. I suppose that's the point, though. Finishing her theme as Madam Xaxu with the ambiance of a gypsy fortune teller who is put in the unfortunate position of telling some poor schmuck why he'll soon be getting fuzzy during each full moon.

"Hold on a sec," Brynne said, opening a cabinet behind a small table. She motioned to a beanbag chair on the floor in front of the table. "Take a seat, Mr. Customer. I'll be with you in the flash of a moment."

"Not for nothin', Madam Xaxu, but you need to work on the consistency of your accent." She stuck her tongue out at me. I smiled and took a seat, looking around her tent. "No kidding, Brynne, this is a pretty spectacular set-up you've got here. I would have eaten this up as a boy. Are those eyeballs floating in that jar?"

She lit three sticks of incense around the tent and then sat down, the small table between us.

"Don't worry, squeamish, they're plastic. I really can read palms, but it's the ambiance that sells. The theatrical touches. Who would you be more likely to believe could tell you the future, Brynne from North Dakota or Madam Xaxu from some extravagant locale in Europe?"

"Honestly? Not to knock your trade but I've never been a believer in any of this stuff – spirit worlds, psychic hoodoo, none of it."

Brynne looked, I don't know, kind of surprised.

"Really? Not even after your past few weeks here in Timberhaven? I figured the Gathering alone would have been enough to shake even the sternest skeptic's doubt."

"I don't know that it's fair to call me a stern skeptic! Particularly with the kind of things I'm taking for truths in this town. Palm reading, conversations with your inner mind, tears in reality covered in psychosomatic bubble wrap – it's just that none of it's a part of my world paradigm."

"Wasn't your last book about a homicidal alien who comes to Earth from a cave on the moon in order to wipe out a near extinct race of, what did you describe them as, light fish? I would've figured your world paradigm to be pretty all-inclusive." She grinned.

"Ah, you're a fan! But they weren't fish, they were squid!" I swooned. "But that's work. I don't believe in what I write. No more than you believe those eyeballs are real. I'm just an accept-what-I-can-see type of guy, is all." I held out my hand to her, palm up. "But I'm willing to listen now. Give me your best pitch."

She took my hand in both of hers but just looked me in the eye for a second.

"Huh," she said and then looked at my hand.

"What?"

"Oh, nothing really. You just sounded a little sad when you said that. That part about not believing in what you write. Anyhow, you ready to be amazed?"

I was enjoying her touch too much to argue. "Let me have it! Is there trouble, Madam Xaxu? Am I destined to go bald and live a life filled with lukewarm book reviews and microwaved dinners?"

She carefully twisted my palm back and forth, tracing the lines in my hand with her fingers like a blind person reading braille. Her touch was electric. Deliberate. I felt completely relaxed as she manipulated the flesh of my hand; played with my fingers. I closed my eyes. Felt as my heartbeat sped. I imagined the blood flowing faster through my veins. I've never had such an intense

reaction to another person. I started to see snippets of light from

behind my closed eyes, like private fireworks, they exploded

within the beats. I felt safe there, with my hand in hers.

Then, I was quickly, painfully aware of a sense of . . .

unease that until then had been unknown to me; one I only

discovered when she suddenly let my hand go.

"I'm, um, I'm sorry." She looked flustered.

I snapped out of my daze and quickly opened my eyes.

"What's the matter?"

"I – I hate to be anticlimactic, but . . . I can't seem to read

your fortune."

I sort of decided to myself that the unease I was feeling was

coming from Brynne, dismissing it away by deciding that I'd

somehow made her uncomfortable.

"Hey, if this is about what I said, I was just yammering like

an idiot. I do that when I'm nervous."

She shook her head. "No, it's not anything you said. I don't

know what's going on. I can always read people. The only people I can't . . . there have only been two people who I have come across that I can't read; Reagan and her father."

I just sat there for what felt like a very, very long time. Even the silence on the tape playback is awkward. I wasn't sure what she was getting at, let alone what I was supposed to say in return.

"I, uh, I don't know what that means exactly."

Brynne just gave a quick, nervous laugh.

"No! Oh, god, no, I just – I didn't mean – I was just saying it's rare that I can't read someone's palm. After all of this build-up, it has got to be somewhat disappointing." She started to get up, so I did, too.

"Well, sure, I was looking forward to –"

I was interrupted by a teenage boy who, nearly out of breath, burst into the tent.

"Ms. Dusayer –" he eyed me and hastily changed it to, "I mean, Madam Xaxu, come quick! They're starting early. They're gonna tear it down now!"

"What?" Brynne yelled. "The legislation was solid! We're voting on it Wednesday. Whistleford gave a stay until Wednesday!"

"Brynne, what's happening?" I asked.

"You better hurry; they've already got a bulldozer there and a big machine with a wrecking ball!" the boy added and then left us to continue his Paul Revere routine.

"Brynne, what's happening?" I repeated as she started to run out of the tent.

"The Citadel! They want to tear it down for parking spaces! Just, come on!" And she ran out with me right behind her.

We ran through the Village and past Old Town, almost all the way to New Town, right to the edge, where a beautiful old theater stood. It struck me like a shot, seeing it there in the afternoon sun, its architect from yesteryear having garbed it in half-remembered dreams of the golden age of Broadway. Looking at the theater, I found it hard to breathe. There was already a crowd gathered around the heavy machinery in front of it, and people were shouting.

"Where's Jesse?" Brynne asked the boy who'd retrieved her.

"Up in the Citadel, talking to that woman," he replied, sneering at the mention of the woman.

I followed Brynne as she made her way through the crowd and up to the theater. My tape is a mishmash of voices garbled together, but Brynne was reassuring certain people as she pushed past them that she and Jesse would get to the bottom of things. At this point, I didn't really know what I was doing there, but I didn't want to leave her.

It was as we entered the Citadel that I remembered, "Wait, Brynne, didn't I read that the town officials couldn't beat the legislation that protected this place? That you'd won?"

Brynne stopped short just before we entered the main hall. I could hear Parson Leets speaking rather loudly from around the corner.

"What are you talking about?" she asked. "We never even got to plead our case, let alone get it to a vote!"

"But the Daily Scroll had a story that –"

"The Daily Scroll?! That's not a real paper, Michael. James Mortimer is . . . he's not well. I – look, I'm sorry to cut this short. I've really enjoyed spending time with you, but can I talk to you later? I've got to see what's happened." She rushed around the corner and into the hall.

Following her, I stopped when I saw who Parson Leets was arguing with. It was Sasha, from the Gathering, seemingly Mr. Trepp's girl Friday. My interest was already heavy with Brynne's involvement. It became all-consuming with Trepp's, so I made my way over after Brynne.

"Oh come on!" Sasha's annoyance is evident in her voice on the tape, "What, is this when you all sit in a circle holding hands around the bulldozers and sing 'Kumbaya'? Give me a break."

"We had until Wednesday, Ms. Clarkson," Brynne replied with ice in her tone.

"Yes, well, Ms. Dusayer, Mr. Smythe never appeared before the notary to fill out his section of the necessary documents in the given time frame. That leaves Whistleford Properties Inc.

well within its legal rights to do with its property as it sees fit, as I was explaining to Mr. Leets here."

"He's an old man, for pity's sake!" Mr. Leets yelled. "You expect him to leave a sick bed to sign on your dotted line?"

"Spare me the melodrama, Mr. Leets. We're done here," Sasha said as she walked away. If she could have, I'm fairly sure that Brynne would have set Sasha's thousand dollar suit on fire with the stare she was giving her.

Just then my cell rang, meaning close proximity to New Town made it possible for Patty to find me. As I fiddled with my phone to ignore Patty's call, I inadvertently answered it.

"Gideon?"

"What is it, Patty? I'm busy." I sighed.

"Yes, yes, well I'm busy too." I could vaguely hear some fumbling about in the background. "I'm at the grocer's trying to figure out their liquor situation. How is it he can't sell real booze here, by the way?"

"Patty, I'm busy," I repeated, frustrated.

"All right, keep your lid on. It's not my fault this selection's shit. I thought –"

I hung up before I heard what he thought.

Brynne and Mr. Leets had come to a conclusion on what they should do next while I was busy ducking Patty. It turned out I was part of their plan.

"Okay, Jesse." Brynne was all business. "See what you can do. I'll handle things in here." Parson Leets headed back outside. "Michael, can you go see if there's any way that Hurd can get here?"

"Hurd?" I mumbled. I felt like I was moving through warm syrup.

"Yes, your neighbor?" Brynne said as she surveyed the hall.

"What, sure, but – what is –"

"We need him to sign the paperwork! As the owner, he can postpone things until we can present our findings and get a vote."

Brynne led us back out to the front door of the Citadel, pushed me out, and shut the door behind me.

"Brynne, wait!" I turned to the closed door.

"Weaver, go!" I heard Mr. Leets shout from behind me. I turned to see him trying to talk to the wrecking ball driver while Sasha tried to argue over him. The crowd was getting louder, half yelling to save the Citadel while the other half yelled to tear it down. The bulldozer driver, clearly on the latter's team, started and revved the bulldozer's engine. I can hear it on the tape long after I'd started running toward Hurd and Angela's place.

Damn. Patty's up. It's time to relocate before he comes downstairs.

*　*　*　*　*

I just met Audrey as she was coming up the steps to my front door. Her hair was simple dishwater blonde now, and she was wearing a gray T-shirt that read *St. Vincent* with *Marry Me* underneath. She was excited about something, as Audrey usually is, and followed me away as I looked for a place to finish posting about Sunday's events at the Citadel.

"It's so exciting, Mr. Smythe being on his feet and feeling better!" Audrey exclaimed, smiling. "And that's in no small part to you, Michael!"

Which brought me up short, stopping both of us in the street.

"What do you know about how things played out last night, Audrey?" I asked. "What, exactly?"

"W-well, I," I had startled her, being so serious, "I know that the Citadel didn't and won't get torn down for a parking lot now, because Brynne chained herself inside while you were somehow able to get Hurd – Mr. Smythe – there in time to sign Ms. Clarkson's paperwork, and now Brynne will get her vote and the Citadel's saved!" She spun, raising her arms up in victory.

"But you don't know – you haven't heard anything about Hurd's recovery? About how his health returned?"

"No, not exactly how he got better," Audrey all but whispered, "just that you were involved somehow."

I thought to myself but didn't respond; I just started walking away from Fallenstar Manor again before Patty interrupted things.

"Oh!" Audrey perked up, reaching into her bag. "As to why I'm visiting, here you are." She handed me an invitation.

"I'm not up for another Gathering, Audrey," I said, looking at the calligraphy on the invitation. "I've got a lot on my plate from the last one."

"It's not a Gathering." She laughed. "It's a birthday! My dad's birthday is on the Fourth of July, and everybody in Timberhaven attends the party we throw at the hotel. We'll have music and dancing, games, cake! My mom used to throw epic parties in celebration years past, but now I handle everything. We're even having carnival rides! Have you ever heard of Goliath? It's a monster Ferris wheel, and we have one for the party! Please say you'll come? Brynne will be there . . ." She let the last part kind of hang there with an even bigger smile.

Even the mention of Brynne's attendance didn't snap me from my thoughts. It's only in playing back the tape that I've realized what she said. I was in another world while she was talking and only responded once I realized she wasn't talking any longer.

"Look, I don't think so, Audrey," I started.

"Well, how about this? I've got to get back to the hotel – there are all kinds of things to take care of, but here, take the invitation," she said, handing it to me, "and just think on it. It's not until Sunday, so keep it in mind."

"All right, okay. I'm going to have to catch you later, okay?" And I walked away into the woods, leaving Audrey no doubt bewildered in the street.

And now I'm sitting here, catching up my journal. I'll apologize to Audrey later, it's just . . . I need to get my mind around what happened after I got to Hurd's place.

I was out of breath when their house was in sight, unaccustomed to running as I am, but I could make out Angela through the kitchen window. She was standing at it, staring out into the yard. It was little Corabeth, though, who was waiting for me at the front gate by the road. She was holding a peanut butter and jelly sandwich in one hand and a piece of paper in the other.

"I need to speak to Angela, Corabeth," I told her, trying to walk around her and into their yard. Corabeth stood her ground, barring my path.

"Hello, Mr. Gideon. Mommy Angela says you can't come in. She says you're still my friend, but that you should know better, coming to ask what you're coming to ask." She took a bite of her sandwich.

"Corabeth, move, please. I need to see Hurd."

She tilted her head to the left a little and looked me dead in the eye, swallowing her bite of sandwich before replying,

"No."

As I debated on how to best get around her without forcibly moving her, she handed me the piece of paper.

"Mommy Angela said I was to show you this if you perstisted."

I took the paper and sighed. "Persisted, you mean."

"That's the word!" she happily exclaimed as I read.

The paper was a note. It was written in handwriting I didn't recognize, yet I was mentioned in it. I read it aloud so I could record it.

"Dearest wife, it is with a heavy heart that I write you this message. Just know that I do all of this to keep you safe from harm. A plan is in place to render this threshold unusable. Gideon will be made Weaver, as we knew he would be, and with his help, Thegan and Leets should be able to maintain the Barrier from widening further, giving Nicoline the time he needs to get his house in order. It is not an ideal plan, but it is solid. For it to work, however, someone must stay and handle things on this side. I volunteered. The others know not to come back here, lest all is lost. You must see to it that none draw me back. This Luminous Knight moniker with the locals should muddy the waters on that front somewhat, as cries for him will not be the same as calling for Hurd Smythe, even if we are one and the same. All you need do is tell any callers that I am sick and can't come to the door. An old man, laid up in his bed is a ruse wasted on the talents of my Lady Actress, so I've no worries there. My concern, as always, lies with your safety. I hope you can forgive me when this is all said and done. I lost you in my own stupidity once. I plan to keep you safe with it this time. Gideon has promised to deliver this to you, my love. He is a good man, deep down, and has been irreplaceable on the front lines of the War these last six months. You can trust him. Ever yours, D"

I shook with rage as I read the words. My time in this town had been draped in madness from the beginning, but this was too far. I threw my tape recorder into the yard of Fallenstar Manor and chucked my journal into the street. My emotions got the better of me and I shoved past Corabeth onto Hurd's property. I wadded the note in my hand as I stormed across his manicured yard; his neatly tended flowerbeds mocked my inner chaos, and I yelled Hurd's name again and again. Quietly at first, my frustration seething, I eventually screamed for the old man to come outside and deal with me. I dared Angela to look out the window at me, dismiss me as she had before, once I'd done what she asked.

I was so angry. Mad at feeling manipulated by everyone here. Mad about not understanding what it was all for. I wanted to hit something, someone. Just to focus on anything other than my own confusion and mistreatment. When I got to the door, I was ready to break it in. One kick, just like in the movies. The door would splinter; the hinges rip. I would drag the old man out of his bed by the head of his hair while Angela screamed for me to stop, but I wouldn't stop. I wouldn't stop.

But I *had* stopped.

I hadn't gotten to the door, nor kicked it in accompanied by a chorus of Angela's screams. Somehow, between the gate and the front door, I had stopped, sat down in the yard, and started to cry. My tears, betraying me fully, dropped onto Hurd's note as I held it shredded up in my hands. I had never felt such anger before, and it scared the hell out of me.

Before I fully realized it, there stood Corabeth in front of me. She had gone to collect my tape recorder and journal from where I'd flung them.

"I'm sorry, Mr. Gideon," she said quietly.

The front door opened behind Corabeth, and Angela came outside to her. She placed her hands on each of Corabeth's shoulders and gently turned Corabeth to face her, kneeling down as she did so.

"What is control?" Angela asked Corabeth with a slight smile, taking my things from her.

"The price we pay for being special," Corabeth answered, clearly a learned response, while tears welled in her eyes.

"You did well, my darling." Angela wiped Corabeth's eyes with her apron. "Mustn't let this upset you. You did very well. Go back inside. I'm sure the cookies have cooled enough."

Once Corabeth ran inside, Angela turned her attention to me. She didn't yell (though I could feel that she wanted to throttle me). She *didn't* hit me. What she did do was offer me a hand up. I stood before her and wiped my eyes.

"You don't know what that note is, do you? Never seen it before?" she stated plainly.

"No."

"I thought not. I thought as much the first time that we talked after you gave it to me." She handed me my journal.

"I never gave this to you," I told her, devoid of any emotion. I was spent. "I'd never talked to you before the other morning in your yard when you asked for my help with Corabeth."

"Good lord, you weren't wrong, my love," a man's voice came from the open front door to the house. A voice I recognized, as it turned out. "He has no recollection of any of it."

"Hello. Hurd Smythe, I presume," I muttered.

"Aye," the old man said. "That's me. Though the question remains, who are you?"

I don't have my . . . reaction recorded as Angela was holding my tape recorder just then, but it was loud and it was intense. I cursed the town, the Gathering, the whole bloody business of being a Weaver, everything. I told Hurd and Angela that I was Michael Gideon, horror novelist and a private person who kept to himself and that I'd had all I could stomach of Timberhaven and its nonsense. It was when I said that child services should be called in to inspect whatever the hell had gone on with Corabeth that Angela slapped me. And with that, I left their yard and went back to Fallenstar Manor.

Patty had met me at the door as I was coming up the front steps.

"What is all the shouting about?" he asked.

"Get out of my house!" I shouted at him as I barreled past. "I'll finish the damn book when I'm good and ready to, and if you don't like it, quit!" I went to my bedroom and slammed the door.

At the time I didn't know if Patty was leaving Timberhaven for good when I finally heard the front door shut behind him, but I didn't care, either. It felt like I was having a nervous breakdown. To a certain extent, it still feels that way. When I'm left alone I can feel the emptiness inside; an unmistakable . . . missing. I can't explain it. It's like a ghost pain, like when someone loses an arm but their brain is telling them that their elbow itches, only it's inside me that something is off.

Why did I have to take that stupid Morpheus Dust and listen to that damned conch shell? If I hadn't, I wouldn't have to deal with the fact that it was Hurd's voice I recognized on the other end of it; I wouldn't have to have these pieces of memory, clips of imaginative morsels that I could write off as bad dreams if I didn't hear Hurd's voice in them.

I sat for hours on my bed, finally succumbing to mental exhaustion and falling asleep. For the first time in a long time, I didn't have any bizarre dreams; only a simple snippet of Brynne and me sipping coffee at a café in some other place. She laughed at my jokes and found me clever when I waxed poetic, and that put me at ease.

I awoke to a persistent knock on my bedroom door.

"I'm in no mood to talk, Patty."

"I am not Patty," Hurd replied from the other side of the door.

"God, go away."

He took that as an invitation to open the door. He stood in the doorway, looking at me. Hurd has sharp features; high cheekbones and flawless skin for a man his age; his striking silver hair kept very short. He's an intense looking man, to be sure, with an almost aristocratic speaking style. If I must have the counsel of old men, I prefer Jarboe.

"What is it?" I asked.

"Might I sit?" He was still standing in the doorway.

"No."

He came in and sat at the desk in the corner, placing my journal and tape recorder on the desktop as he made himself at home.

"I have not been here for some time," he told me. I didn't answer, so he continued, "This room used to be beige and have posters of teen heartthrobs hung about; that Michael Fox fellow and the like." He looked around as he talked. "It is a bit boring, now, I suppose, in contrast."

Something about a man his age discussing teen heartthrobs struck me as so ridiculous that I smiled involuntarily. Making me lighten up hadn't been his intent, evidently, because he just kept staring around the room and then back at me, his discomfort apparent in his lack of knowing what to do with his hands.

"What can I do for you, Mr. Smythe? As you know, it's been a trying day for me."

He cleared his throat. Then he cleared his throat once more. After clearing it a third time, he stood back up and walked toward the door, stopped, and then turned back to face me.

"This, as you have probably gleaned from my behavior, is difficult for me, talking to you like a stranger when we are not strangers. I am uncertain as to why you are . . . different now, so I do not know the proper stance to take, conversationally speaking." He fidgeted.

"Why don't you just sit back down and answer me one question?" I asked and waited for him to be seated back at the desk before I continued, "Why do I recognize your voice, have strange memories that you're in when I only just met you?"

He took a long time in answering, staring out the window into the woods as he weighed his words.

"You do not recall . . . any of it? The War? The Valley of Half-Formed Monsters? The truce made at Bekinsdraught?" He looked at me, disbelieving, as I tried to control my emotions.

"No. No, you are talking nonsense."

"It is not nonsense!" he bellowed, standing again. "It has been my life these past three years! I kept to the plan, I did! Then I get word that you have not only come back through the Barrier but are wandering around its borders like some youth on a field day. Fool!" He knocked the chair into the wall.

"Calm down!"

"I will not! You came to us, a savior born of prophecy and prayer, only to deliver us to damnation!" He was on me before I knew what was happening, holding me by my shirt. "Why do you not know any of this!?"

"Get off!" I pushed him, hard, away from me, and he stumbled back, slamming into the door frame. For an old man, he can take some roughhousing, but he merely shook it off and stood there, looking at the floor and collecting his composure.

"I apologize," he said, looking up at me once more, "I did not heed my wife's advice. She said I needed to keep my head, and I have decidedly not done so. I will try speaking with you again later if you will allow it. Good day, sir." And he walked downstairs and out my door as I sat there, adrenaline pumping and my thoughts a maelstrom of chaotic energy.

Brynne came later, overjoyed that I'd gotten Hurd to the Citadel in time, saving it for another day thanks to his timely arrival, and hugging me in thanks for that. I wasn't in the mood for visitors, and she left but only after she made me give her a rain check for a night on the town. I made her leave feeling unsure about me, I know, but I don't know what to do here in Timberhaven now. Patty came back, unfortunately, but kept to himself the rest of last night. This entry is very long, I know, Evey, but it may be my last. I felt the need to tie up all the information I got yesterday. I planned to be finished with this; the journal, weaving, Timberhaven, all of it. My head is not – I'm not in a good place right now. It's like when you died, only . . . this time there's too much confusion in my mind about what's real and what isn't.

I had planned to be done like I said, so I ripped a blank page from my journal and wrote Patty a note – *We're leaving. Pack up and be ready* – and I put it on the couch. I walked out of the manor with my journal, not knowing where I was going exactly but with the plan to dispose of the journal. I was going to leave it behind with this crazy town. I didn't even look toward Hurd's house as I left. Screw him. Screw all of this. I don't need this. That's what I was thinking.

I decided to throw my journal into Shadow Lake, just outside of town. I found the little rowboats that you can borrow and tote around the water in, and a burial a sea, such as it was, struck me as perfect.

It was closing in on sunset when I arrived, but it was still light enough out for me to see two people sitting at a little picnic table not far from the water's edge. It turned out that I knew both of them and, unfortunately, would need to walk by to get to the boat.

"Well, Christopher, look who it is. Michael Gideon, the local celebrity," Bernie said my name sarcastically, quickly signing to her tablemate with her hands as she did so.

C.P. smiled up at me and waved his little boy wave. I almost hadn't recognized him without his violin. Bernie took his hand away gently into both of her hands, drawing his attention back to her.

"No, no," she said as she continued to sign. "You are far too cool a kid to waste your time on such a serious stick in the mud."

My quest to get rid of my journal and to be done with everything here in Timberhaven was completely interrupted by Bernie being *kind* to someone. She wasn't even cussing every other word! I just stood there, kind of in shock while C.P. signed something back to Bernie.

"Okay, okay. Not kid. I meant little dude," Bernie returned. "Anyone can see you're not a kid." She pointed over across the way and then continued, "Hey, it'll be getting dark soon. Go get your violin from Kings Park, and let's get you home."

C.P. hopped up from their bench by the lake and ran toward another bench that was placed near topiary of life-size chess pieces. Bernie stood up in front of me.

"What the hell's your problem, asshole?" she asked, returning to normal.

"I don't have time for this, excuse me." I moved past her to the nearest boat and started loading it into the water, remembering why I was there.

"Hey, psycho, what are you doing?" she yelled. When I didn't answer, she walked away mumbling to herself.

I had started to climb into the boat when I heard it, C.P.'s violin. Once again I was stopped cold by the music. I froze, drinking in his song like a marooned man dying of thirst, finding bottled water. That piece of music he played, so full of hope, of life, it framed the moment amazingly. The sun going down, the wind on the water and the birds in the trees; I'll be haunted by the perfection of that one moment until the end of my days.

At some point, I had walked from my half-deployed boat and over to Bernie and C.P. while his song played only realizing I had done so once he stopped. He was doing a sign, his left arm out while his right hand seemed to be swatting flies away from his inner left elbow, and whatever it meant made Bernie smile until she saw I was there.

"No way, little dude," she told him. "You know our deal. Besides, this guy is a . . ." And whatever I was, she had only signed it, making C.P.'s eyes go wide as he smiled.

C.P. waved goodbye to me after putting his violin back in its case, and the two made off. Bernie didn't say another word.

Kind of lost, I stood and watched them leave. Emotionally, mentally, I was so tired. Finally, I went and sat down on the bench in the topiary park, nearby what I think was a Knight. Suddenly I saw a puff of smoke come from behind a Bishop.

"Hello?" I called out. "Who's there?"

A silver-haired man walked from behind the bush, leisurely strolling along toward me in dress pants, a white dress shirt, and tie. His tie was loose and his sleeves rolled up; he had his suit coat slung over his shoulder.

"Oh, hello." He smiled at me. "I didn't realize anyone else was here. How does this evening find you?"

"I – uh, hi. Hello." I flushed for a moment, as this guy had yet another voice that I recognized, though I'd never seen his face, and for a moment I thought I was dealing with a second Hurd situation. But then I placed his voice.

"Mr. Fell?"

"Oh!" he said, extending his hand to me. "I'm sorry, we've not been introduced. I'm Jacobi Fell. Mr. Fell was my father. And you're Mr. Gideon. You and I spoke briefly on the phone as to arrange your stay. I hope Audrey has been able to help you on that front."

"Yeah." I nodded, releasing his handshake. "She's been very helpful."

"Enjoying our town?"

I didn't know how to answer that, in the mix of emotions that I was having, so I only nodded and looked back to the chessboard topiary. "It's interesting all right."

Jacobi laughed. "That's one way to put it, given the situation you've found yourself in. I can't imagine it's been helpful insofar as seeing your book finished."

I must have looked perplexed then, because he continued, "Oh, yes, I know that I look New Town, but I grew up in Timberhaven. My heart is in Old Town."

"You certainly aren't given to speak in riddles like everyone else here. It's refreshing."

Jacobi reached into his coat and retrieved a sandwich bag full of raisins, offering me some before saying, "People in Timberhaven, more often than not, have been living here all of their lives. They've got a sort of shorthand, a way of being and interacting with one another that they sometimes take for granted around new folk, that's all. They don't mean anything by it."

"I've been here nearly two weeks. They picked me as Weaver in less than half that time. You think they'd be as little ambiguous as possible." I had started fiddling with my journal, gently slapping the cover.

"You were done, weren't you?" he asked, looking at my hands. "Going to destroy the journal and leave town, just pitch it all in?"

I tried to mumble something, but he waved me off.

"It's okay. I understand. Who wouldn't, being an outsider, given how eccentric Timberhaven is?"

"I'm sorry." And I was, too. "I – I had an episode. Things aren't making sense in any real-world sort of fashion here."

"Can I ask? What stopped you destroying it?"

I didn't hesitate. "The boy's music."

"Christopher Philip?"

I nodded.

Jacobi smiled. "The child is a joy. And his presence comforts Bernadette. Or so it seems."

"He's an amazing little boy. I've never heard anything like what he can do. And seeing Bernie being kind to someone! I haven't seen that since meeting her."

"It's a shame Christopher Philip couldn't get her to sing for you. There was a time when she was quite renowned for the beauty of her voice."

"Really? Her grandpa must have loved that. Too bad she's so awful to him now. The only thing I've heard her voice is a string of profanity."

"Ah, yes. She's got quite a wit, always has. She and my Audrey have been nearly inseparable since they were babies." Jacobi looked lost in thought then. "The fallout of her relationship with her grandfather is quite sad, but she hasn't been the same since her father, Timothy, passed. Lord Jarboe hasn't either. Some families are blessed, you see, having *many* lights – family members who can balance the darkness and downtimes, reminding the rest of us that it's all going to be okay just by their being alive. If those families lose any one light" – he looked off onto the lake then – "the spirits of the other members can still be buoyed by their remaining lights. Other families . . . are not so lucky."

I suddenly felt very sorry for Bernie then. And also like I had stumbled into a solemn situation, so I changed the subject back to what I'd witnessed prior to Jacobi's arrival.

"C.P. is – I don't even know. That song he just played? It moved me. And the fact that he can't hear it himself, and yet creates it. To have faith in his instruments, that he's making music, with no way of knowing for sure. And, I mean he can't even tell for sure that Bernie's, I'm sorry, that Bernadette's actually really singing with him. It's beautiful."

Jacobi looked at me, puzzled. "Well, of course, she's really singing."

"Well, no, I know she is, but, you know, being deaf, there's no way that *he* could know, too. Not for sure."

"He knows by the look on her face as she sings." Jacobi smiled. "The glow that comes from connecting to one's gift in such a manner that you can no longer doubt that in all the wonders of this life, I am where I am supposed to be. Doing exactly what I am *supposed* to do. He can tell by the look on her face."

He stood up to leave, tipping a salute at me as he did so.

"Where are you going?" I asked. I felt a kind of warmth inside myself. I wasn't ready to be alone with it, or at the very least, didn't know what I should do next.

"You have a decision to make, and I must leave you to it. But know this: as we visit here, you, Michael Gideon, are our Weaver," he said it with conviction, with weight. "Now whether you remain and do what needs doing, I don't know. Maybe part of being Weaver is that you need to decide what that means to you. I can't tell you. But I do know that there is much work to do, and the cause is noble." He stopped to put his raisins away. "Audrey keeps me in these to help me stop smoking, and damned if it's not helping. Well, I've cut back, at least." He slid his coat back on and made to go. "If you need to call it quits as Weaver, be done and go. Those in the know here will understand. But you *are* who Timberhaven needs, Michael, that much has been decided. Being needed, that's a heavy thing. Some people can hack it, others can't. Which kind are you?"

And with that, he left me sitting there with my thoughts.

I got back to the manor to find that Patty hadn't found my note yet. I threw it away and told him goodnight.

There, it is decided.

I didn't dump my journal in the lake.

I'm not going to leave Timberhaven.

I'm their Weaver, and right now that means my making sense of the playing field so I can make an informed decision on what to do to help here.

I think I should start with Audrey Fell.

*   *   *   *   *

June 29, 2010

Patty won't leave Timberhaven, but he says he'll leave me alone more if I can at least show him some progress on the book and we can have booze in the house.

And something besides pears.

Hard as it was to get into writing mode on the book, I knocked out three pages last night. Enough to keep Patty busy, I think, while I go out this morning.

Audrey was too busy to talk with me today unless I didn't mind talking with her while she saw to some of the decorations for Jacobi's birthday party. I can hardly keep up with that girl.

Just now, on my way to meet Audrey, I saw one of the children-like monks again, standing at the forest's edge across from my porch and staring at me. Well, staring toward me, at any rate. (I can't say for sure, what with the hood being up.) I had only made out what I was seeing, the blond ringlets peeking from under the hood, when, once again, there was nothing there.

I don't have time for more mysteries . . .

*   *   *   *   *

When I found Audrey at The Fell Hotel, she was not alone.

A motley crew of children, some I knew and a couple of fresh

faces – a pale little girl with a long brown ponytail and a dark-

skinned girl who was gesturing excitedly at a book the two poured

over while they tucked themselves away under one of the small

party tables set up around the courtyard, and two little boys who

were leaping chairs and chasing around after Reagan – and Audrey

was trying to get all of their attention.

"Give me two seconds, Michael." She hurried, turning

toward the kids. "Okay, OKAY!" That got them all to look at her.

"Thank you for helping set up the tables and chairs, my lords and

ladies, but I think it's high time you all found someplace else to

play, preferably somewhere not underfoot."

Little redheaded Reagan started running again, and the two

boys – they all looked to be about the same age – chased after her.

Her ever-present playmate Corabeth walked over to me from her

seat at one of the tables.

"Hello, Mr. Gideon."

"Hello, Corabeth." I looked back to Reagan and the boys. "You don't want to play with the others?"

"I don't understand these games," she said, following my gaze as well. "Alekos and Jake just chase after Reagan, and Reagan *wants* them to chase us, and Juniper and Maya keep going on about Maya's book about the nighttime stars. Stars in books aren't very interesting to me."

Then a thin, tired-looking woman with sandy blonde hair tied up haphazardly on top of her head came out into the courtyard. "I've got the inside tables all squared away, Audrey. I need to get Alvie fed some lunch now, but I'll be back downstairs after."

"Oh, Penelope, thank you!" Audrey ran over and hugged Penelope quickly before she was off again, straightening tables and chairs, but then quickly mouthed to me, "I'll be right back" before running inside.

"Alvie, let's go get some lunch," Penelope yelled, trying her best to be heard over the squeals of Reagan.

"Nice to meet you, Alekos," Corabeth said, offering her hand to the little boy who ran over to Penelope. He just looked at her like she was the weirdest thing he'd ever seen.

"Alvie Harrison, shake her hand, young man," Penelope said.

Alvie did as he was bid and the two made their goodbyes, with Alvie muttering something to his mother.

"That's your name, child of mine," Penelope told him. "Alvie is only your nickname. Her calling you by your proper name is not weird, and shaking hands is being polite! You should try it some time."

With one gone for lunch, it seemed that all of the kids were now leaving, until it was only Corabeth and Reagan mulling about. Reagan climbed up on the five-foot-tall rock wall that separated the courtyard from the outer grounds and bid Corabeth to follow her.

"Now, be careful, Reagan," I said. "If you fall, your mom will have my hide."

Reagan balanced her arms out to her sides, with Corabeth mimicking her, as the two walked along the top of the wall. Without looking at me, her eyes on her feet, Reagan innocently asked, "Do you like my mom?"

I could feel myself blushing. "Sure, I like your mom."

"But do you like Reagan's mom like Jake likes Reagan?" Corabeth asked from out of nowhere, all the while staring at her own feet.

"Corabeth!" Reagan yelled, laughing as she jumped down from the wall, running toward the outer grounds and out of sight.

"Where is she going?" Corabeth asked, genuinely confused, as Audrey came back out into the courtyard.

"Why don't you go and find out?" I couldn't help but smile, thinking of the secrets of little girls.

She hopped off of the wall and made to follow her friend.

Audrey came back out with a huge stack of tablecloths so tall I couldn't see her head. I did, however, see that she was about to trip into one of the chairs not pushed in under a nearby table.

"Audrey, look out!" I needn't have bothered yelling, though. You can hear the thump on the tape as the obstacle chair flipped across the courtyard into the wall leaving Audrey safe from any harm.

I still can't believe what I'd seen. Even as she set the tablecloths down and asked me what was the matter I was standing there trying to make sense of it.

"I – okay, you, Audrey." I took both of her hands in mine and led her over to a chair, effectively seating her. "You just sit down and start talking to me. The other night, the bottle, the beer bottle – the beer bottle Bernie threw went end over end over – and then, before it hit your face, it went whoosh! Away from you to crash somewhere else and," she tried to interject something then but I just keep going, "*and* then the chair, that chair" – I pointed over to the wall – "was here, and you were about to trip and so I yelled a warning but then BAM! The chair is not here but over there, and physics is physics, but physics is *not* physics here in Timberhaven, and Audrey, what the hell?!"

I think I handled that pretty well, all things considered.

"Well, Mr. Gideon, Michael, it's not that –"

"Audrey," I had to interrupt. "Chair."

She took a couple of seconds, a deep breath, and relaxed before she started,

"I've always been lucky. Anytime, ever since I was born to hear my parents tell it, anytime I would have gotten physically injured, something happened that made it to where I wouldn't be. It just didn't happen. Case in point: bottles changing their mind mid-throw – though, to be fair, Bernie didn't mean to throw it at me so much as at Lord Jarboe, and it slipped – and chairs going out of their way to get out of mine when I'm trying to carry too much."

She said it just like that, too. Like bottles and chairs flinging across the room to keep you out of danger was just the most normal thing. I opened my journal and flipped through its pages until I found my list. I slammed the journal on the table, startling Audrey.

"Look, I – I'm sorry." I ran my fingers through my hair. My naturally wavy curls were getting a bit thick and unruly, and I had a stray thought then deciding that I need a haircut. "I'm – uh –

I think that a person can only have so many nervous breakdowns in a set amount of time, and a few weeks is certainly too small amount of time so, w-we're going to take a beat, slow things down, and we're going to discuss, you and I, this list of – putting aside the chair and the bottle thing – this list of questions I have." I smiled, hoping that it was a happy-looking smile and not a serial-killer one.

Audrey returned my smile and looked at my list.

"I'm number two!" Her eyes lit up.

"Yes. You're number two. Now, Audrey, I've come to discover that Timberhaven keeps no secrets from you. . ."

I left it there, and she thought on this for a second, until she finally said, "I'm not sure that I know *every* secret . . . and besides, just because I know something doesn't mean it's my place to talk about it, to share."

"That's completely fair." I tried to calm us both down, though Audrey is kind of unshakeable so it was mostly me who needed calming. "It is. But maybe if you *do* know something, you could give me a hint. Or maybe point me in the direction to figure it out on my own. I need help, Audrey. None of this makes enough sense to me."

She quietly looked over my list once, then again. "Well . . . number one is easy enough. You could ask around to nearly anyone in Old Town and discover that the forests surrounding us here in Timberhaven have a rich history – even back to the days when the Native Americans, the Abenaki tribe, first settled here. Something out there is alive, or can at least call forth things that *were* alive," she said it straight-faced, too, not a hint of joking. "It can also bring things – people too – that were only ever alive in dreams before, in stories. It can make them real. But only within the borders *of* the forest can these walking dreams come to life. I don't know all of the ins and outs, just the main idea."

I figured screw reality; I'd play this like a local. "So, you're saying that the reason I feel a tug whenever I walk in the forest, you're saying that that's because of characters I created waiting to, what, be born? Come to life off of the page?"

Audrey sighed. "Basically, yes. But not just any character. It has to be one fully imagined; completely. Also, it has to have been put down on paper and you've got to be open to the forest while walking inside of it."

I started to pace in front of her, the whole idea, imagined people and things coming to life in the woods if one was open to it. I flipped the idea back and forth in my brain like a terrified bird stuck inside a closed room. If I believed this ridiculous story, and I didn't think Audrey was lying, I needed it to make sense without any holes in Timberhaven logic. (Since clearly real logic needn't apply within the city limits.) I had remembered Inari the one time – vividly, sure – but it wasn't like I saw her or anything. The monk children I've *actually* seen – the blond one twice now. But I never – children are missing in *Chaos Fair*, but I haven't formed any of their characters nearly close enough to fit what Audrey's describing here. Besides, the first time I saw them wasn't in the forest, but on my front porch! No, Audrey wasn't helping with number one on my list.

"Let's move down the list," I told her.

"I'm sorry." She seemed genuinely upset. "I'm not doing this well, am I? Nothing I'm saying is helping you."

I ignored her apology. I felt very – something was, is, wrong. With my thinking, the way I'm dealing with Timberhaven. And the Why of it all is right in front of me if I could just get some of the nuttiness out of my line of sight and look at it clearly.

"How about Hurd, there, number three?" I stopped pacing and sat down at the table across from her. "I hadn't met him, but I knew his voice once I did meet him. How does that work? In the real world, I mean. Who the hell is Hurd Smythe?"

Audrey looked at the list and then looked me in the eyes. She was sorry, I could tell, but I needed her to talk. "Mr. Smythe – well, all of that, really – has to do with the Barrier and I'm the *last* person you want explaining that to you. Thegan is your man there."

Thegan. I could hardly understand him on a good day with his talk of colorful bricks and circles in the dirt. It would take my witnessing something astounding in these woods to make me talk about the Barrier again, with Thegan or anyone else for that matter. The idea is just too big for me to buy into, a tear in reality? I can't take it on faith. I can't just believe.

I need proof.

"Okay, fine. But Audrey, help me out with one, in particular, some solid help." I pointed to number four. "You're the only reason I know anything about Dorthea and the singing on Thursdays." Which isn't entirely true, as I had heard Thegan whisper Dorthea's name at the Gathering, but I needed something to start the ball rolling here. "Point me in the right direction."

"Okay, but then we're done telling stories that aren't mine to tell here. Fair?" she asked, standing up as she did and offering me her hand like we had just made a bet.

"Sure, what choice do I have?"

"All right, here it goes. Fallenstar Manor, before I was born, belonged to Samuel and Margaret Nicoline. Samuel is a doctor – not a medical one, but physics – and Margaret was a homemaker. She would have made a gifted architect, too, I think, because she designed Fallenstar Manor, and I think it is the most beautiful building in Timberhaven, outside of the hotel, but I'm probably biased. I mean the hotel's stained glass windows on the third floor alone." She was getting back to her normal ratta-tat-tat speaking pattern.

"Audrey, Dorthea?"

"I'm just about to get there." She took another big breath. "Margaret got pregnant with Dorthea. The pregnancy was very rough from the beginning and, unfortunately, she died having only just seen her daughter come into the world." Audrey looked down at her hands before continuing, "I think that's why I've always felt a sort of connection to Dorthea. It's a hard thing, to lose a mother, and the idea that – I mean to not even have known your mom. I can't imagine not having the chance to know mine. Dad is great in every possible way, but still. I miss my mom every day."

I didn't coax her along again. Instead, I let her take her moment.

"So, yes, Dorthea was born and, by all accounts, grew into a talented young poet and a beautiful young woman. Did you know she's the youngest Weaver Timberhaven has ever seen? That's amazing talent. We haven't had a Weaver since her, until you."

"No? What happened to her?"

"The last night she was seen, it was a Thursday. There was a dance at the high school. She went with Austin Woodthall, a boy that people say she was destined to marry. They danced to her favorite song –"

"Let me guess," I interrupted as it clicked for me, "Freddie Jackson's, *You Are My Lady*."

Audrey smiled. "Yes, very good! Anyway, Austin said he walked her home and that was the last time anybody ever saw her. They searched for months and months but didn't ever find her. Dr. Nicoline couldn't handle the loss, which some say is strange because he hardly seemed to notice Dorthea when she was around, but I think it's just that he lost his daughter and the last physical connection to Margaret all in one go. Either way, he went a little . . . funny after that night, and that's when Lady Nicoline started making appearances. He sold Fallenstar Manor, a name that the people of Timberhaven christened it with in honor of Dorthea, to my dad and we've owned it ever since. You weren't the first renter to hear Dorthea happily humming her favorite song, though. It's like she's living that lovely Thursday night forever. Isn't that wonderful? Oh, I've got so much to do! Hope that helped, Michael!"

And she was off again inside the hotel. I came back home, looking at Fallenstar Manor differently than I had before. So now it had a story to go with the name. It's a sad story with plenty of holes – they never found her body? Did they arrest Austin? Question him? – but at least I learned something from my list. Do I believe it? I hear a song on Thursdays. That much I know.

I'm sitting on the porch, catching this all up. Patty went to the store and got more booze. He liked my new pages for *Chaos Fair*. This morning seems like a lifetime ago now.

I'm going to eat a pear.

*   *   *   *   *

Oh god.

Reagan. Little red-headed Reagan has been attacked.

I don't know much other than they found her at the edge of the woods near the hotel. Some . . . monster had been hurting her roughly fifty feet away from where Audrey and I had our conversation. It happened so close – right there. Her clothes were ripped, and she was barely breathing. They've got her at Timberhaven's urgent care facility where she's still unconscious.

Brynne had gone out looking for her once it started to get dark and Reagan hadn't come home, and that's where and how she found her daughter.

Once Audrey made it known that she and I were probably the last two to have seen her, Sheriff Vindego of Timberhaven stopped by the manor, with Audrey in tow, and asked us if we had noticed anyone else around where the kids were playing at the hotel this afternoon. Unfortunately, we couldn't give him much help, wrapped up in our discussion as we had been at the time of the attack, aside from the fact that she had been playing with Corabeth.

That led the three of us over to Hurd and Angela's place, and there's where we found out that Corabeth hadn't come home either.

"Hurd is out looking for her," Angela explained to the sheriff, meeting us at her front door, her eyes puffy and her face flush, "and has been at it for an hour or more, once it had become dark. Corabeth knows to be back before dark. He would not let me leave to help in the efforts, for obvious reasons, so I am left to wait here for their return. Did Reagan say where she'd seen her last?"

"Angela," Sheriff Vindego began, his hat in his hand. "The little Dusayer girl was found outside the woods by The Fell Hotel. She was . . . she's hurt."

Angela stiffened, leaning against the door jamb.

"She's not woken up yet," the sheriff continued, "and the doctors down in urgent care think it's best to keep her sedated, for now, keep her resting. That being the case, we don't have any idea where the two might have gotten off to from where Mr. Gideon and Ms. Fell had last seen them. You haven't by chance seen either of the girls talking to anyone –"

The sheriff was interrupted by Angela collapsing to the floor. He caught her just before she hit. Audrey and I helped stand her back up, and the three of us got her seated on a small couch just inside the doorway.

"I'll sit with her," Audrey said. "We'll wait for word together," she said the last to Angela who was looking pale with worry.

"Thank you," Sheriff Vindego told her. He turned to talk into the little radio hooked on his shoulder.

"Are you okay, Angela?" I mumbled, kneeling beside her. A stupid question, but helplessness makes for stupid dialogue.

"Please go, Michael," she nearly whispered. "Help find her. Bring her home safely to me."

I promised that I would. The second promise I've made to this woman without knowing the situation.

The sheriff left to go gather more bodies to help look for Corabeth, and I'm jotting this down while I wait for Patty to throw some shoes on so we can join in the search. I feel so damn helpless, so guilty; this, writing it all down, it's the only thing I can do to keep from punching the wall.

*   *   *   *   *

It's a little after midnight.

I'm sitting on an old chair at urgent care, drinking coffee that tastes like it was filtered through a stripper's bra after a hard night's routine, from a paper cup that I would swear used to contain old change.

We haven't found Corabeth yet. It's been six hours, and there are at least twenty people looking, Mitchell included, but so far nothing. I wanted to stop by urgent care. I just left Brynne at Reagan's bedside. Not surprisingly, Brynne doesn't feel much like talking. She squeezed my hand and thanked me for being there, asked about Corabeth, but that's all. Brynne's got no vitality about her. It's like she's using all of her energy, willing her child to wake up. Reagan. The poor kid would look like she was only sleeping if not for all of the tubes, IV, and the beeping monitor.

We picked up Mitchell not long after leaving the Smythe residence. Sheriff Vindego had to stop by the station to organize the volunteers there into search parties, and that's where I saw Mitchell, looking into a jail cell and talking to Hudson through the bars.

And Thegan was sitting in the cell next to him.

I walked over, dumbfounded.

"Thegan?"

He was slumped down, his massive arms leaning on his legs with his face in his hands. He looked very tired.

"Michael," he spoke softly. "It's an awful thing that's happened." With that, he put his face back into his hands.

"They're both POI," Mitchell told me, leaning over to whisper into my shoulder. "Persons of interest. I don't think Vindego believes either of them had anything to do with –" he swallowed hard, taking a couple of seconds before continuing, "Mostly that your guy there – Thegan, was it? – has some kinda history with the little girl who's missing and Hudson, well, nobody likes a new face in town when something like this happens."

I remembered, then, Thegan's reaction to Corabeth at the Gathering. I don't know him well, but I can't imagine him actually hurting anybody. As for Reagan . . . to hear Brynne tell it, Anthony Thegan would walk through fire for that girl.

"How is it you're not in there with them if that's the case?" I asked, shifting gears in my mind.

Mitchell looked taken aback, that laid-back cool face he always wears flashing from surprise to hurt.

"Ouch, man." He looked back into the cell. "I alibied out. I was . . . busy, with Bernie." He pointed over to the front desk where some poor desk jockey was being explained to by a very loud, very upset Bernie that there was a little girl hurt and another missing and it seemed that the speed at which things were moving along in the searching for said missing child was not happening quickly enough to her liking.

"Sorry," I told Mitchell, "wasn't meant to sound as accusatory as it did. It's only – I know Reagan and her mom a bit. Corabeth, too, and it's just an awful thing. All of this."

Sheriff Vindego was handing out flashlights, breaking everyone up into groups, when Mitchell said, "So let's go and find the missing kid and get her home. Let's find one ray of light in this horror story."

After about an hour of looking our search brought us by the urgent care and I decided to come in and check on Reagan.

I can't understand a person who would hurt a kid. What kind of sick mind it takes to –

The robed children were right in front of me; all five again, standing and staring from beneath their hoods, with little blonde ringlets standing as leader. A nurse came into the room and didn't react to them at all, and there's no way Audrey could have missed them on my porch the other day, so now I know that I'm it.

I'm the only one seeing them.

One at a time, they each began to point at me, little fingers on little hands from beneath the folds of their robes.

They slowly walked past me, still pointing, heading down the hall.

Toward Reagan's room.

I ran for Brynne and Reagan. I don't know what I thought I could do, but I wanted to protect them. When I got there, Brynne was asleep, holding Reagan's hand. No little ghost children to be found.

"You're going to have to leave, sir," a stocky nurse harrumphed at me. "Visiting hours for non-family members are long over."

She was glancing at me with an "I'll Call Security" look, so I put up my hands in an "I Give Up" gesture and walked away. What the hell does this mean? I'll worry about it later. I'm taking a second to jot this down and then I'll follow Security Nurse's less than subtle suggestion. I want to check in on the other searchers anyway, to see if they found Corabeth.

* * * * *

It's all over now.

I . . . I can't do this yet.

* * * * *

July 1, 2010

My tape recorder is gone, destroyed in the chaos of the last couple of days. That's a terrible way to start this entry, but I need to start somewhere.

I came back to the manor that night after leaving urgent care, only to find it turned completely upside-down. The couch was flipped over; the books knocked from shelves, my clothes were strewn about, just wrecked. There were noises coming from the kitchen so I cautiously stepped to the corner.

There was Patty, rifling through the cabinets.

I was so confused, I blurted out, "Patty?"

He jumped at his name and spun around, looking to pounce on me. Seeing that it was me, though, he brought himself up short, wiping the sweat from his forehead.

"Michael!" He smiled, looking me over. "I really, I've got this bottle of wine, and I really need to find an opener. Have you one?"

I turned away, looking around the place at his spectacular mess. "What the hell, Patty?"

That's when I felt a small stabbing pain in my shoulder. I caught Patty in the corner of my eye right as he injected me, and I pushed him away, hard. He looked so worried, standing there stuttering apologies as the world started going fuzzy.

"Of course, you have it on you. Of course, you do." I was seeing two of him then, and they both wore fuzzy flesh-suits. "I can make this right, Michael," he said, as if to a child. "You've just got to stay out of my way. Now, give me your journal."

I tried to fight him off, but I was no match. He took my journal from me as I fell to the floor, flipping through it rapidly while I lay there.

"Pa-Patty?" was all I kept saying until there was only drool and the promise of sweet oblivion. Patty's voice started to sound further away, but I could make out a little.

"The dark-haired little one, I can't find her. She has to be – I need her to not say anything – what she saw me do. I'll handle this, and then things will get back to normal. We'll get out of this damn town! Need her to be quiet. I'll quiet her."

And then, I was released.

*   *   *   *   *

I was in a room, next. It didn't belong to me – I was thinking at the time that I couldn't remember the last time a room had been mine – but a friend of Patty's. I was so, so drunk, which felt good. Normal. Like that was how life was meant to be lived, loaded and feeling no pain, feeling nothing but the buzz. I'd missed that feeling.

A sense of the familiar started to set in. I'd done this before, been wasted in this room after a book signing. Where had it been, Denver? Seattle? I realized then that I was dreaming of a memory. A hazy memory, given my resting pulse of stupid drunk, but still, there it was. I tried to focus, but intense pain came with even the idea of trying to.

My head was down on a desk or a table, and though I wasn't looking at it, I could feel the glass in my hand. I had closed my eyes in the memory but found that I could force them open in the dream. God, it hurt. There was a sound then, a voice. I recognized that voice.

Patty.

"It's quite all right, my dear, you needn't cry." His kind assurances in the dark. "Patty will make it all okay."

I heard him open the door to the room I was in and tried – the pain was unbearable, forcing me to close my eyes – to turn my head his way, see what was happening. I hadn't done so in the memory, so doing so in the dream was impossible.

Or it should have been.

"Gideon."

I didn't know where the voice was coming from, saying my name.

"Gideon!"

It irritated me, this voice, barking at me. What do you want? Why does everyone pull on me? Can't I just enjoy myself, drink and make merry? I missed being how I used to be; like Mitchell. Who's Mitchell? That young guy I met in Timberhaven, remember? Timberhaven? You know, where I went to finish my book and . . .

"Gideon, damn it!"

That voice. It was Hurd's voice. I turned my head toward the sound of it.

I opened my eyes.

There was Patty, trying to quietly open the door into the bedroom so as to not disturb my drunken sleep. There was Patty, whispering quiet assurances in the dark. There was Patty, holding a clearly drugged little girl in his arms, wrapped up in a blanket and looking like a midget monk.

She had little blonde ringlets peeking out from the corner of the blanket.

I cried as the bedroom door closed behind them. I cried in the dream. I had done nothing in the memory.

How had I not seen what Patty was? How did I not know? How many signs had I missed or ignored while I spent so many nights in so many cities wasted? How many times had I been *right there* and not done a thing?

Oh God, how many lives, how many children –

And that's when it clicked: the robes, the pointing, my seemingly nonsensical visions in Timberhaven.

I *have* been distracted by a secret.

But not one I've been keeping consciously.

It had been five times.

Five children.

Little redheaded Reagan made six.

The next thing I knew I was in a field on a moonless night. My dreaming memory had ended and the pain with it. I heard galloping from somewhere in the darkness. I couldn't get my bearings, everything felt off. I chose to focus on the sound of the galloping.

"Be ready."

Hurd's voice cut through everything and that's when I saw the light. It stood out in the darkness like a star going nova.

"I'm coming."

And the memories flooded. I felt dizzy from them. They came in bundles without context. Hurd and I, inside the Barrier. Talking. A war, a terrible war.

How had I forgotten?

"Here."

The Luminous Knight was upon me, his arm outstretched for mine to pull me up. I was aware, awake at the edge of dreaming, and I knew what I had to do.

"You know I am unable to offer further assistance?" the Luminous Knight said beneath his gleaming light helm. "My duties prevent it."

I knew. We rode toward a reddish-blue light at breakneck speed.

"Just get me back. I'll figure it out."

We rode through that reddish-blue light, and I woke up.

I woke to the sound of light rain tapping on the roof of the manor. I was sluggish with jellied arms and legs. It wasn't until I saw my journal lying on the floor in front of the kitchen that I fully snapped to.

Corabeth.

Patty.

I crawled to my knees as the world spun, causing me to puke up my pear from earlier. My head throbbed, making it difficult to process my thoughts, but for the first time since I arrived at Timberhaven, those thoughts were clear.

Patty needed to find Corabeth to shut her up about what he'd done to Reagan, only he'd lost track of her and didn't know where to look. Hell, a squadron of people hadn't found her yet. But I remembered, then, where she probably is.

And I had written it down in my journal a week ago.

I made my way as quickly as I could (which is to say I was swaying and stumbling a lot) outside. My head was still wonky, but I was pretty sure I remembered how to get to the Dragon King throne.

Once I made it outside, the cool rain helped clear my head a little bit. The sky lit up occasionally with lighting, like fireworks showing me the way. I saw Hurd in his yard, right where I knew he would be, now that I remembered some things. Angela stood just inside the open front door. She gently kissed her fingers and waved me on as I stumbled past their house toward the woods.

I came upon Sheriff Vindego and a couple of other people, none of which I recognized, helping to look for Corabeth just as the lightning started to pick up. A thunderbolt clapped.

"We're going back for some suitable clothes," the sheriff yelled over the rain. "We're not giving up yet!"

"Follow me!" I yelled back. "It's Patty! Patty did this! He's going after the other girl, after Corabeth, and I know where she's hiding!"

That was enough to get everyone moving quickly again, as well as we could through the forest. Whatever Patty had drugged me with seemed to be slowly wearing off, but my vision was still a little cloudy, and at that point, the rain getting heavier wasn't helping matters.

I kept thinking, as we all tore through the forest, about the five other children. In truth, even though I didn't realize it before, I guess I've been thinking about them since I started writing *Chaos Fair*. It took Timberhaven to show me the truth.

There came a point, once we found the trail that the girls had used the other day, where I began getting further and further ahead of the others as we took the path to the giant tree. Someone fell down, tripped, like in a horror movie. Only instead of running away, we were running toward the monster.

"Don't do anything unless it will keep the little girl safe," the sheriff warned as I began to distance myself further. "I'll handle things with your friend."

My stomach turned at the mention of Patty being my friend, but I ran on ahead.

The lightning lit up the sky once more, and then again. Thunder boomed as the rain fell. The path was a muddy mess as my feet sank a little bit more with each step, making it impossible to run. I could just make out the trailhead right in front of me. There was Thayne's throne.

I didn't see Patty or Corabeth anywhere.

I got to the tree, looked up and around it, and just then, I caught movement going up the cliffs toward the gorge. Patty was scrambling, as well as his weight would allow him to, up the cliff side and there, near the top, stood Corabeth.

"Patty, stop, it's over!" I yelled, but my warning was lost in the thunder. I looked to find the others but found myself standing alone.

I tried to make it up the cliff after them, knowing even as I started that I wouldn't make it to them before Patty made it to Corabeth. She was stuck at the top with nowhere to go but into the chasm over its edge.

"Patty, no!" I yelled again, but he shimmied on up the muddy cliff, indifferent to my shouts, a crushing wave of destruction aimed at a little girl.

I haven't told anyone what happened next. Even though I have some memories now that allow me to make a little sense of Timberhaven, this is still the really real world. My eyes could have played tricks, or maybe it was the last of the drug Patty injected me with causing an intense last-minute hallucination before it quieted in my veins.

But I know it wasn't.

I'm the Weaver, after all.

The crunching sound of the tree falling behind us, as if a giant were climbing from its bed, was the only accompaniment to the piece, the coda to my story that I hadn't seen coming. How could I have?

Patty had reached Corabeth well before I could. Mud was seeping down the cliff side in sheets. The thunder roared, highlighting the murder of this little girl to the soundtrack of angry gods. The lightning . . . the lightning flashed, the storm exploding the sky in a brilliance that it had yet to reach until that point despite its best efforts. Everything was bright, for a flash of seconds, and as I looked, as Patty raised an arm to Corabeth to crush her, wiping her from our lives with a blow, it happened. The dark, black storm clouds behind them changed shape in the light show. All at once, as though they'd only been pretending until then, those sweeping dark clouds ceased their form.

They became a monstrous dragon, hovering above the scene like a glorious nightmare.

Even in the noise of the storm, I could hear Patty scream as the arm with which he had raised to knock Corabeth into the gulch twisted, an insane effort to protect himself against the inevitable, as the dragon's toothy maw clamped down around him. Only his legs above the knees were visible then, kicking, squirming as a worm cut in half might do. There, its massive wings flapping to keep it aloft above the gulch behind Corabeth, the dragon lifted its mighty head, opened its throat, and finished the meal that was Patty.

As I fell to my knees, stunned, slipping and sliding down the muddy embankment to its base, I remembered the night that I'd met Corabeth and how I had discounted her overactive imagination as we walked her home to Angela:

I like your forest. Do any monsters live there? I have a dragon named Thayne. He likes to catch monsters. He cuts them to ribbons and gobbles them up!

I regained composure enough to see Corabeth sliding gingerly down the cliff toward me, the storm clouds in the lightning only storm clouds again.

"Are you okay, Mr. Gideon?" she asked politely.

"I'm – I'm fine, Corabeth. Are you okay?"

"I'm kind of hungry, a little bit," she said, taking my hand and guiding me down toward the path. "Can we go home now?"

At the base of the cliff, by the collapsed great tree whose remnants would now and forevermore belong to Thayne, the Dragon King, we found the rest of the party that made up

Corabeth's "rescuers". The sheriff bought my story (weaving fiction into facts gets easier the more one does it, apparently) that Patty had fallen down the gulch while attempting to attack Corabeth, and he suggested that we should get Corabeth home and everyone out of the weather.

"We'll see about collecting his body once this storm clears. I don't hold out much hope, though. That gulch goes on and on," he said as we walked back to town.

"Yeah," I agreed. "I don't hold out much hope either."

The storm, powerful though it had been, stopped nearly as quickly as it had started. Once we finished up back at the police station after Hudson and Thegan were released from the holding cell (Thegan left abruptly without a word to anyone), Sheriff Vindego drove Corabeth and I home. None of us talked much on the way to Hurd and Angela's. The sheriff let me walk Corabeth to the door and headed back to the station. Hurd was still doing his dance around the yard. Angela hugged Corabeth tightly when we got up to the porch.

"Oh, child, I am so sorry."

"I'm not hurt, Mommy Angela." She pulled back from the hug to look at Angela. "But Thayne maybe did a bad thing."

"I will see to it that Thayne gets a score of sheep for what he's done this night," Angela told her, tears in her eyes.

"Can he have butter peanut and jellies instead?"

Angela smiled. "Whatever he wishes, my dear. Now, if you go inside, I have laid out something for you to eat. You must be half-starved. Go ahead. Hurd and I will be in shortly."

Corabeth smiled and ran into the house, stopping just at the door and turning back around.

"Is Reagan going to be able to play tomorrow?" she asked me.

"The doctors are doing everything that they can, dear," Angela interjected, "to see that that poor girl wakes up again. Run along inside and eat."

Once Corabeth left, Angela shocked me by resting her hand on my shoulder.

"Thank you, so much, Mr. Gideon," she said, showing just how scared she had been. "Thank you for getting her back home to me."

"I'm to blame for her being in danger to begin with," I said, turning from the porch, exhausted. "It's the least I could do."

Angela was quiet for a second before saying, "It is not your fault."

"It sure feels like it is."

We stood quietly for a few moments, the events of the night weighing on us. Finally, I made my goodbyes.

"You came back to see me, to give me his letter the night of the 18th," she said, looking to her husband who seemed oblivious to us in the yard. "You came back in full command of your faculties. Whatever happened to make you . . . less, happened after you left here."

I didn't respond. I found then, as I fidgeted it out of my pocket, that my tape recorder was finished. Whether it happened when I fell to the floor after Patty drugged me or in my scaling up the cliff, I can't say, but it was destroyed.

"It is refreshing," Angela continued, "being able to speak with you clearly. Though, you still seem off, not yourself. Hurd is concerned, and so am I."

I didn't look back to her but instead kept watching Hurd as he rounded the corner of the house again. "Nobody in town knows," I began, ignoring her comment, "that the Luminous Knight they so adore, all of his protection allowing them to sleep better at night, that it's all of it a result of his love for you, do they?" This time she didn't respond. "That's an epic love, Angela, from the novels of old."

"Well, *our* novel ended differently," she offered, sourly, to my unintended pun. "And there's no need to romanticize it. What Dorian –" she caught herself, "what Hurd does, it comes from a place more complex than love. I still cannot believe he told you. You are the only person from this side who knows. There are those here that if they knew who we truly are, the ramifications . . . but no. We *can* trust you, Mr. Gideon. You two certainly *must* have bonded during your time together inside the Barrier."

"Well, with six months over on that side, it left a lot of time to talk." I smiled. "I mean, we couldn't be planning war strategy all of the time."

"He's a man of many secrets, your husband, and I don't pretend to know them all," I said, walking across the yard toward Fallenstar and ending our conversation with a yell back, "But I will keep those I do know, this one in particular. Have no fear."

I came home. It was too late to go back to Brynne and Reagan, and I didn't have the nerve anyway. I knew that Brynne might have heard by now who attacked Reagan. That it was Patty. I noticed the bottle of vodka on the bar next to the bottle of bourbon. Patty had restocked after all.

The bastard.

I'm finding it hard to see the man he was, the monster, in the man I knew. It won't fit in my head. Timberhaven, for all its insane ways and eccentric townspeople, got hit by a snake that I brought with me, and I need to make that right.

Somehow.

It's been a day now. High past time to find the stones to go face the music.

*   *   *   *   *

~~For the first time in nearly a month, I'm drunk. Drunk as I write this. I'm sitting in the dirt in The Village watching Brynne's tent burn. Madam Xaxu left. I took away her baby girl, and she hates me now. Can't say as I blame her.~~

~~I hate me too~~.

*   *   *   *   *

Neither Brynne nor Reagan was in her room at urgent care when I arrived. I asked the stocky nurse from the other night, and she told me that Reagan had been transferred to a hospital out of town and that no, as I wasn't family, she couldn't tell me which one.

I walked back to the manor and grabbed the bottle of bourbon. The top came off smooth, like a silver-tongued mistress whispering sweet nothings. I took a swig and almost puked it right back up. Keeping it down, though, I took another swig and decided to go for a walk.

I caught up to Brynne in her tent as she was packing the last of her things into a large suitcase. Her back was to me when I opened the tent flap.

"Brynne?" I put my bottle down on the ground.

Her shoulders sank, but she didn't turn around. She just kept packing all of the little tell-tale signs that Madam Xaxu worked there into her suitcase.

Finally, she started talking, "Audrey is going to watch the boutique for me until Reagan gets better" – the tears that she'd been hiding, I realized, started to come out again – "until I know when Reagan can leave the hospital."

She put the suitcase down and tried to clear off her cabinet of an oil lamp, the only source of light in the tent now that the flap was closed, but stopped, putting her hands up to push me away when I approached to help.

"Michael, no, just . . . no, please."

"What can I – I only want to help. How can I help?"

That's when she finally looked at me, tilting her head to the side as tears streamed down her face. "I know," she choked.

"Logically, I know that none of this is your fault. That my daughter" – she turned away again – "that Reagan isn't unconscious with the doctors having no way of knowing when she'll wake up, that none of that is because of you. I know that." She reached up, trying to untie the top of the tent to begin breaking it down, but the knot wouldn't give. "But I can't. Every time I see your face or even think your name" – she tugged, frustrated at the tie down – "it leads me to think of *him*."

She screamed then. She grabbed the oil lamp and threw it against the side of the tent. As it smashed to the ground, it lit the oil, causing the tent to catch fire, but she calmly picked up her suitcase and headed for the entrance.

"I don't need anything else," she muttered, and we left the tent as it burned.

I watched as she walked away, flames licking her tent until it was fully engulfed. She never looked back. Other people started running around trying to put out the fire while I sat down with my bottle of bourbon and watched it rage.

The other people, performers and artists, they got the fire under control fairly quickly. Brynne's tent was done for, but the surrounding settlements were in no danger. A few people tried to shout at me to help with the situation, one or two checked to see if I was all right, but I just sat there drinking until everyone went away, leaving me with Brynne's fire.

Finally, a man's voice called me back from the flames.

"Audrey said you'd be here," Jacobi said, walking up the path toward me.

"She always knows," I slurred.

Jacobi sat down next to me but didn't say anything, only watching the dying fire with me.

We sat there for quite a while, but I eventually interrupted the tent's whispering smolder.

"I'm so . . . broken." I swigged some more bourbon. "I truly am."

"We all feel that way at some time or another. Particularly times like these."

I wasn't hearing that, though, in my state. It wasn't enough. "Sure, sure. I know. But do people put their faith in you? I bet that they do. I bet that you spin your folksome wisdom and fix it all for 'em. But that's the downside, ya know? It's a crapshoot. Sometimes damaged goods will rise above, save the day. Underdogs!" I drank some more. "But other times . . . well, that's the danger of placing your faith in broken people." Another swig from the bottle. "Good intentions don't make it hurt less when you get let down."

Jacobi took the bottle then, startling me as he did, and then he drank long and deep from it, watching as the tent burned. The smoke from the blaze blotted out the evening sky above Timberhaven like a faulty pen dropped into an aquarium.

"Faith," Jacobi finally said, "for some folk, is a dangerous thing. Too much keeps them from taking responsibility for themselves, from doing the work at hand. Too little, they lose hope; they figure 'what's the point?' and turn bitter. Useless." He took another long drink from the bottle before handing it back to me.

I was exhausted. I sat the bottle down. "So what do I do, then?" I asked, staring back into the fire. "How do I make this right?"

"This?" Jacobi asked. "I'm not sure it can be set right. But sitting here, being 'broken', that doesn't seem to be a worthwhile cause. Being broken is easy." He stood up, taking the bottle with him. "Being better, that's the challenge."

He left me sitting there. I stayed until Brynne's tent was nothing but ash. I watched as that ash flitted up and away. I rose with it, standing, nearly sober by then and walked back to the manor. After a few hours of sleep on the couch, I woke up to a mist-covered Timberhaven, grabbed a pear, and sat down to write this.

I've seen enough. I remember enough to know that this is where I need to be right now – where I'm supposed to be. I've always found that phrase juvenile, the oft-wished feeling of the overly romantic fantasist. But every choice in my life, every event, every person, place, and thing, even and especially you, Evey, has led me to this moment, this place. So it's the only phrase that covers how I feel. I don't have all of the answers that I need, but I know where to look. It's time for long, patient conversations with Hurd, with Lady Nicoline, with Thegan. No more monsters are getting by on my watch.

No more.

Timberhaven *is* that room of my own. It's my place of belonging. And I protected it without even understanding what I was doing when a tale I'd woven for some children on a cloudy day reached down and ate the last monster who threatened us.

But now I understand.

Timberhaven is home.

And I am its Weaver.

Here's an excerpt from when

Timberhaven returns in:

Juniper Soot and The Monsters In The

Park

Coming Soon!

*   *   *

Juniper and Jake had hidden Slow's guitar near a giant rock that they had found together at the beginning of the summer, burying it under sticks and leaves the best they could. Dirt, Juniper thought, might damage the guitar.

Then, to Jake's delight, they were headed back out of the forest.

"There's still a monster, you know," he'd kept mentioning as they walked.

The edge of The Fell Hotel's property, and thereby the northern edge of Old Town, was contained in a high, red stone wall standing eight feet tall. Above it, iron bars with spear tips on the end of each. Juniper and Jake walked along the base of the wall, running their hands along the artwork graffiti that was painted all over it. Bridges and buildings were drawn there, from all around the world and other worlds, too. An ugly troll fought a gallant knight under a banner of silver oak here, while a rocket rounded a red moon there.

Juniper loved examining the intricate details hidden all over the wall. Or would have, had Willoughby not lived there.

Jake's eyes filled with joy as he looked all over, scouring the artwork for a sign of the first and only real bit of Timberhaven's magic that he had ever seen.

Willoughby was a chalk drawing who typically stood no more than two inches tall, though he could grow and shrink as he liked, of a little man wearing a purple shirt with a dragon on it, a California highway patrolman's helmet, big sunglasses circa the 1970s, and huge, gray swimming flippers. He also happened to talk, and he moved endlessly around the collage, so one never knew where to find him.

Juniper stopped and took off her backpack, checking around to make sure no one could see them. She sighed and then looked up at the drawings, trying to catch some movement.

"Willoughby," she whispered. "Willoughby, come out here, it's important."

Jake looked back and forth at the wall, smiling.

"Willoughby," Juniper said a little louder.

"Say, *Sir* Willoughby," a tinny little voice said from somewhere on the mural, but Juniper couldn't pinpoint it. Jake giggled.

"Hush, Jake," Juniper said. She squinted a double-take at a clockwork Labrador's eye but hadn't, it turned out, seen Willoughby there. "Willoughby, we need help."

"You know the rules," Willoughby's voice came again.

"Enough, Willoughby," Story said from Juniper's backpack, with a slight meow of encouragement. "We haven't the time."

Suddenly the faceplate of the knight fighting the troll came up. "Sorry, Story," Willoughby said, his voice no longer tinny. He popped from the knight's armor onto a mermaid from a merry-go-round painted under a starry sky. "Didn't see you there," he continued, giving the mermaid a giddy-up. "Happy to be of service."

"Neat!" Jake exclaimed.

"Jake!" Juniper shushed him. "Willoughby, we need to ask you something, and we'd like a straight answer."

"I've only crooked answers, but there's a hammer over there," Willoughby pointed to a Viking warrior landing a crushing blow with a war hammer onto an unfortunate demon's head, "that you could probably straighten them out with."

Juniper sighed. Willoughby was always difficult, but he was way worse when it came to her Juniper thought.

"Willoughby," Story said.

"Apologies, but I don't get many visitors these days and I do like to talk," Willoughby smiled, having teleported to a race car at eye level with Juniper. "Ask away, Doctor Soot," Willoughby often playfully mocked Juniper's love of science.

Jake laughed and tried to touch Willoughby's face peeking out of the race car, but Willoughby had already popped back up and was perusing something that a man in a 1950s style office building was typing out.

"Jake, stop," Juniper said. "You're as bad as he is," she looked back up to Willoughby. "We are looking for our friend and we were wondering about a monster that may have come into New Town."

"Alas," Willoughby said. "I can answer but one question per customer."

Juniper thought for a moment. "Okay, where's Slow."

Willoughby stammered, thrown off by Juniper's quick decision, but then sat on a drawing of Rodin's The Thinker, mimicking the pose.

"Your friend . . . I'm sorry," Willoughby appeared in front of Juniper's face again. This time he removed his helmet. "But your friend is in two places at one time."

Juniper's face went ashen. "Is, is he dead?"

"That is not for me to say," Willoughby bowed. "But rarely, if ever, is it a good thing to be in two places at once," he thought again, and added, "you need to go see the giant killer, in name if not action, for what to do next."

"I don't know what that means!" Juniper yelled.

"Juniper, calm down," Story said from the backpack. "Thank you, Willoughby. Juniper, we'll figure it out. Make your payment."

Juniper picked up a stick of charcoal from the many that were scattered around the ground in front of the wall. She drew in, poorly, a pair of black socks, with the left one having a hole in it, on the mural.

Willoughby harrumphed, but still inspected the socks with a smile.

"Okay," Juniper added. "Your turn, Jake."

Jake smiled, and then yelled. "WHAT'S THE MONSTER THAT ATE MY PANTS?"

"Wait, what?" Willoughby said, thinking their business concluded he felt quite bewildered.

"You said one question a customer. Jake's up next," Juniper smiled.

Willoughby admitted his defeat with a sigh. "Fine, fine," he scrunched up his face. Then, if drawings could go pale, Juniper was sure Willoughby was doing so. "The creature is not of this world. It's not – it won't be sated with a small taste like before, no. It has been stuck these many years. In between – in a hole with a view – to get to nibble but never bite. It hungers. It hungers so much."

Juniper shivered. The thought of the thing from Jake's picture being real scared her.

Jake had been drawing a baseball and glove on the wall while Willoughby explained things and finished up his drawing with a master's focus. He already knew that the monster that had eaten his pants was real, after all, and so could get no more scared of it than he already was.